Soul Survivor

a novel

Edward Steiner

SOUL SURVIVOR

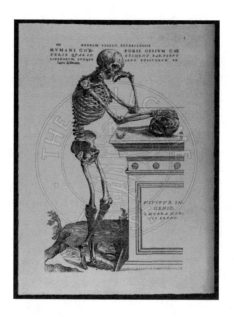

Edward Steiner

A Vitruvian Book
Published by Data Trace Media Inc.
Towson, Maryland

Published by Data Trace Media, Inc.
P.O. Box 1239
Brooklandville, MD 21022-1239

All rights reserved. First Edition, February, 2004
Second Printing, April, 2004
Printed in the United States of America

Library of Congress Cataloging-in-Publication Data

Steiner, Edward 1956–
 Soul survivor / Edward Steiner.
   p. cm.
 "A Vitruvian book."
 ISBN 1-57400-094-2
 1. Human experimentation in medicine—Fiction. 2. Death row inmates—Fiction.
 3. Transmigration—Fiction. 4. Immortalism—Fiction. 5. Physicians—Fiction. I. Title.
 PS3619.T47625S68 2004
 813'.6—dc22
                          2004041335

DEDICATION

I would like to dedicate this book to my three children, Lauren Ashley, Brittany Leigh, and Brandon Scott. Their inspiration, interest, and visualization of this work through the innocence of young eyes was a wonderful experience.

I would especially like to dedicate this novel to my wife Dana, who has helped my true "soul survive." She continues to do so with grace and beauty.

ACKNOWLEDGMENTS

I would like to thank Dr. Herb Fried, Cindy Lee Floyd, and Data Trace Media Publications for their help in the publication and copyediting of this novel.

I would also like to thank Shelley Morhaim for her productive comments and for her intense dedication in co-authoring and writing the screenplay based on this novel.

CONTENTS

For Tantalus was the favored mortal son of Zeus, and as such, was the only mortal allowed to partake of the food of the Gods—but Tantalus abused this gift by revealing to mankind the secrets he had learned in heaven. He angered the Gods, who forever cursed his very existence.

—The Oracle of the Gods, Damocles

PROLOGUE

MOLDAVIA, 476 A.D.

THE OMINOUS room was dimly lit. The glistening, rough stone walls seemed to weep fluid, and hundreds of candles flickered throughout the cavernous space. There was very little furniture—a stark desk, a wall shelf filled with small religious items, and two large granite pillars flanking a stone altar with a flat marble top resembling an operating room table.

His name was Svintu. Like many medieval words, his name had a dual meaning. In some sentences the name meant Angel, in others it meant Devil—the Evil One. This was not, however, unusual. The Dark Ages were difficult for most people, and the distinction between evil and good was often one of degree and not substance.

Svintu was the sorcerer, the healer, and the soothsayer. His eyes were deep and penetrating. It was difficult to gaze into them without looking down in reverence. He dressed in a long black robe with no ornaments or ceremony. His powers lay in his "sorcerer's ways," in his eyes, in his control of the situation.

In the small Romanian village of Piatra, the castle of Count Ghiorghiu overlooked the countryside with an ominous presence. Rock and stone denoted power when most Moldavian villagers lived in small thatch roof huts. Svintu was the Regin, the power behind the count. He was the throne, regardless of royal ancestry.

The peasants told tales of his powers and spells. Misha knew of these tales and knew he was dying. He knew his only hope was an audience with the Healer, the Regin, Svintu the sorcerer!

For a man riddled with the consumption, Misha climbed the castle stairs leading to Svintu's chamber with vigor. Svintu rarely accepted an audience, and this was Misha's only chance. As he arrived at the sanctuary door, he knocked gently at first, then a little louder. The door was fifteen feet tall. The knocker was an enormous brass ring held in the teeth of a brass lion's head.

"Your holy worship, may I enter the chamber?" asked Misha, slowly opening the chamber door, palms sweating with both fear and anticipation.

There was silence for a moment, followed by a whisper. No—not a whisper in the literal sense, but a near silent response, mysteriously amplified to the loudest shout Misha had ever heard.

"You may enter the chamber and approach me!" said Svintu in a tone neither harsh nor demure. A tone that spoke control and power. A tone rehearsed for decades.

"I have brought you a gift—an unworthy gift, but all I can give," said Misha, raising a slaughtered chicken in the air. As Misha slowly approached the altar candles, his features became visible. He was gaunt, consumed by disease, his eyes yellow with jaundice, his bones barely covered by leathery yellow skin.

"You may leave your gift where you stand. Come up and lie down on the altar. I do what I do, because it is what I do. My healing powers lie in the earth. My healing power is granted by the power of the earth itself, by the minerals within its breast. By the northern rocks I call magnetite. I shall place these magic stones upon your body and they shall cleanse your humors of your jaundice and disease. You shall go home a cured man, but only if you believe in my powers, Misha!

"Do you believe?"

CRATHES CASTLE, SCOTLAND, 1989

The Burnett Clan owned the land on which Crathes Castle was built. The castle itself was built between 1550 and 1600. Scottish haunted castles have become a staple tourist industry, and Crathes Castle is one of the most famous.

Nobody actually knows who the ghostly Green Lady was; however, it is believed that even Queen Victoria witnessed her apparition while visiting the castle. As legend has it, the ghost is the spirit of a lady who brutally murdered the lord of the castle upon discovering his indiscretions. She had just given birth to their firstborn.

The Duke had both mother and child executed to avenge the death of his son. Since then, the Green Lady has glided across the haunted birthing room. She appears and floats towards a cradle next to the fireplace. She then gently picks up her infant and suddenly both apparitions vanish.

It took three years for Professor Abernathy Jones of the Georgetown University Department of Particle Physics to get permission to bring his setup to Crathes Castle. His hobby-turned-research was the scientific evaluation of the paranormal.

His doctoral research into particle physics was conceded to be brilliant. Jones was a tenured professor single-handedly responsible for mathematically describing the interaction of two black holes within a billion-mile radius. After the Hubbell telescope confirmed his theoretical equations, Jones rewrote the basis of the origin of the universe.

Some people drive little sports cars as a hobby—Jones hunted ghosts. Georgetown tolerated his eccentricities as a necessary evil.

It took six hours for Jones and his team of paranormal enthusiasts to set up their equipment. A television crew accompanied them from the Discovery Channel, filming a special on paranormal activity.

"Could you describe your equipment for our watchers, professor?" asked a young female broadcaster.

The professor loved putting on a show. "What you see here is some of the most sophisticated EMF activity detectors in the world. Forgive me—EMF stands for 'electromagnetic flux.' Most experts on the paranormal believe that ghosts, or "entities" as we call them, are electromagnetic in origin. When these entities appear, they not only interact with static fields, but also actually disrupt them in a measurable way. This is the 'tri-field extended range meter,' a device originally designed to read the activity of geomagnetic storms. It is so sensitive that it can pick up even the fields of living persons. We put three of them in this room and then we can triangulate and actually detect motion vectors.

"This particular meter can actually pick up electrical and magnetic readings simultaneously—it's called a SUM setting. We also have an ELF or "extreme low frequency" meter by the fireplace and a tri-field extended range meter on either side of the room, designed solely to pick up motion.

"Behind you, we have a wide-angle infrared camera used in Vietnam to detect the slightest heat signature—all standard ghost-hunting stuff, you know!"

The broadcaster really didn't know what to say next. She asked for the Afghanistan assignment and she got "The Absent Minded Professor Meets Frankenstein"—until the meters started going off!

1
TESLA 6—WALTER REED ARMY MEDICAL CENTER

THE RHYTHMIC KNOCKING of the MRI machine at Walter Reed almost drowned the conversation outside the magnet. Captain Jake Eriksson was on duty, accompanied by the chief MRI technologist, Sergeant Emanuel Rodriguez. Rodriguez was raised in the Bronx and joined the military right after DeWitt Clinton High School, his way out of the ghetto. He was career military and enjoyed his job. Some of the doctors were assholes and treated him like shit, but Jake was a nice guy. They could have real conversation, the kind that bonded men of all classes together. That rare breed of testosterone-laden machismo present in country clubs and slum bars alike.

"What's shaking, Rodriguez?" asked Jake as he entered the MRI suite.

"Just serving my country!" answered Rodriguez. "Gotta real VIP in the scanner, Captain. Master Sergeant DeMarco's wife. General Kovalik has been down at least three times. Mrs. DeMarco's CT scan showed a liver mass. One of the other radiologists thinks it's a benign hemangioma, but General Kovalik wants to make sure it isn't spread from her breast cancer."

Jake stared at the preliminary and saw no mass. He looked at the prior CT hanging on the viewer behind the scanning console, and the scan definitely looked suspicious for tumor to him. MRI should be more sensitive than CT.

"Rodriguez, change the standard scanning sequence and do an inversion recovery pulse as the next scan. This lady's screwed—looks like tumor on CT," said Jake, fingers slowly tapping the front panel of the MRI console.

"Captain, our usual sequence is a T2 sequence for hemangioma," responded Rodriguez with a look of worry on his face. The last time he and Jake went on a scanning adventure, General Kovalik, the Medical Director of Walter Reed, had his ass handed to him on a platter.

"Listen, Manny. Our pulse sequences are remnants of the stone age of MRI. Kovalik's staff developed them before Dr. Hahn published his landmark articles on abdominal MRI at Harvard. I was his senior fellow—I should know! Kovalik doesn't know shit about MRI."

Jake was brilliant but arrogant. He had been brought up in one of the wealthiest families in Boston. Marblehead was home during the school year, a house on Martha's Vineyard during the summer. School always came easy to him. Harvard undergrad, a brief excursion into aerospace engineering at MIT before he decided medicine was for him. He liked the concept of playing God. It was about the only thing he had not experienced. Those shows on TV always glorified the stressed-out residents, fighting with the attending physicians to do the right thing for the patient. Saving lives—he could see doing that as a career.

Women were always a commodity to Jake. They came and went. He never really cared. Kind of like buses, another would arrive in fifteen minutes. His reputation was probably well deserved, and he did his best to keep it up in medical school as well as in the military. Rodriguez liked that about Jake. A male bonding thing. When you have four kids and a Roman Catholic wife, you tend to live vicariously.

"Well, I'm glad you have such a high opinion of your commanding officer and his staff!" shouted Kovalik, who had been standing behind him for at least two minutes. "Assholes like you make me sick, Captain. Your daddies run out of money and you decide to get a free ride through medical school on Uncle Sam. Well, I got no free ride and barring your arrogance, I happen to have the best MRI radiologists in the country—do you understand, Captain?"

"Yes, sir!" responded Jake, with the old "I'm fucked" look on his face.

"Did you deviate from our routine T2 protocol on the sergeant's wife, Captain?"

"Yes, sir, but for tumor the IR sequence—" Jake could not even get the next word out before Kovalik's explosive outburst.

"Son, do you know what an Article 32 is?" asked Kovalik.

"Yes, sir, an investigation or hearing pending court martial, Sir," answered Jake.

"Well, let me give you an education in Subchapter Ten of the Uniform Code of Military Justice. You see, I may know nothing about MRI, but I know just a little about handling Ivy League shits like you. Article 88 is 'contempt toward officials'; Article 89 is 'disrespect toward a superior'; Article 90 is 'willfully disobeying a superior officer's command'; Article 92 is 'failure to obey a regulation'; Article 108 is 'wrongful use of military property'; Article 115 is 'malingering while on duty'; Article 117 is 'provoking speeches or gestures'; Article 133 is 'conduct unbecoming an officer and a gentleman.' Now, there are 146 Articles and I have each one of them committed to memory—do you know why, Captain?"

"No, sir," answered Jake in a demure voice. He held his pose in military tradition, eyes forward, focused at an arbitrary point on the wall in front of him.

"So I can take arrogant spoiled little shits like you who never earned their captain's stripes in battle and nail them to the wall. You see, Eriksson, this is not a democracy. I am your commanding officer. You WILL do what I order! You WILL go where I send you! And if you ever disrespect me again, you

WILL be cleaning toilets in the DC Veterans Administration
Hospital—or getting butt-fucked by the inmates in Fort Hood
in Texas, DO YOU UNDERSTAND?"

"Yes, sir, I apologize, sir!"

"That's better, Captain," smiled Kovalik with the most
incredible look of self-satisfaction. "Now what does Sergeant
DeMarco's wife have in her liver?"

"Tumor," said Jake with a quiver in his voice. "The CAT
scan only showed one area, but on the IR sequence her liver is
full of disease."

"Too bad," responded Kovalik. "Sergeant Thomas
DeMarco served in Nam with me and is one of the finest
men and one of the most decorated noncommissioned officers
in this country. I'll tell Tommy myself."

After Kovalik left the room, deadly silence persisted for
minutes. Rodriguez knew this was coming. He just hated
being there when it happened. Jake had been pushing Kovalik
on MRI protocols and the Tesla 6 project ever since his reassignment from Fort Bragg. Walter Reed had the only 6 Tesla
magnet in the military, and Jake wanted to do research on it.
There were only four such magnets in the world.

Jake had already published articles on a Tesla-3 superconductive magnet at Mass General, but the T-6 was different. An
experimental MRI deep in the bowels of Walter Reed, generating a magnetic field six times that of conventional MRIs.
This MRI magnet generated a pull 350,000 times the magnetic
pull of the Earth. Yet to be FDA-approved, once it was activated, even trace metals in clothing would be pulled into the
magnet with such force that a human would be crushed like
a grape. Patients and the technologists had to wear special
paper gowns. The running joke was that any human accidentally stuck in the magnet would look like the house Cabernet
wine.

"I dunno, Captain, seems that this was probably not the way to get on Kovalik's good side," smiled Rodriguez. He would never say that to any other officer, especially after the reaming Jake got, but he had gotten to know Jake pretty well. It was the comic relief they needed to break the ice, and Jake appreciated it.

"Well, I tell you, Manny, fuck 'em if they can't take a joke—that's what I always say," smiled Jake. There was a twinge of worry in his eyes.

"Cheer up, Captain, Lieutenant Carlson is coming on duty in 15 minutes. She always seems to get your plumbing started."

"Susie 'the Sub' Carlson—love to get a few minutes with her in the magnet," smirked Jake.

"Don't get yourself into trouble, Captain! She's a maneater, that one. I've seen her devour officers with more stripes than you. Besides, I think Colonel Smith has a thing for her," said Mannie, rubbing his chin. "You know that Kovalik's going to tell Smith your opinions of his pulse sequences. Don't think Kovalik didn't notice how easily your IR sequence showed Mrs. DeMarco's tumor. He respects your knowledge; he just doesn't trust anyone who is not 'pure military.' You have to go through basic training. You know—break the man down before you build him up bullshit. Kovalik is a good officer. A Vietnam hero. He's the President's best friend and personal physician, for Christ's sake! Watch your ass and play it smart. You'll get on the T-6 project, but play the game."

It was very good advice from Rodriguez. It's just that Jake had this thing about women! Call it a defective Y chromosome. As Lieutenant Susan Carlson entered the MRI suite, Rodriguez knew that his speech had been wasted.

As he exited, Jake bent down to whisper to Manny, "You know, Manny, a praying mantis knows his mate will decapitate him and eat him after sex, but he still goes for it!"

Susan smiled at Jake, sensing they were talking about her.

"And that's why the mantis prays, Captain," whispered Rodriguez. "And just like the mantis, you haven't got a prayer—a maneater—remember!"

Susan Carlson had only worked with Jake on two previous occasions. After the first, she pulled some strings at the Personnel Office and got everything the military had on him. She knew that all she needed to do was bat an eyelash, but that's not how a professional predator works. Part of the fun was stalking the prey.

Jake would be a challenge. Not to bed, heaven knows it took an average-looking blonde about three seconds to induce lust in even a "happily married" married male. Susan knew that Jake would be worthy game, especially given his reputation and academic drive. She enjoyed the cat-and-mouse routine. The cat always plays with the mouse a bit before the final kill.

Besides, his wish to enter the T-6 project was well known. Manny and Susan were the only two technologists trained on T-6. This gave her an added advantage. She loved using different-flavored bait.

"Jake," said Susan. "You don't mind me calling you by your first name, Captain, behind closed doors, that is." Susan's smile said slightly more. Somewhat inviting but just enough to maintain a professional attitude should Jake choose not to pick up on the line.

"Please, Susan. I'm not brass. Just putting in my time and trying to save humanity in the process. Besides, you can call me anything—'behind closed doors,' that is!" Jake was smiling devilishly.

Susan wondered if Jake was kidding or if he really had as high an opinion of himself as everyone said. It didn't matter to her. He looked like a young Clint Eastwood. She was sure he had enough bullets in his .44 Magnum!

"Keep it holstered, Romeo! I'm just making pleasant conversation," smiled Susan. This time, the smile had a totally different meaning. She knew she won round one. "Besides, what's a silver spoon preppie like you really doing in the military?"

"Well, it's a long story. The short version was that Daddy could probably buy the Tesla-6 research magnet. He was proud as can be when I got into Harvard. He pushed me into MIT after my undergrad degree. I never liked engineering—almost failed computer programming in the first semester, but ended up nailing the final test. Quantum physics and relativity, now that got me off! I guess that's what attracted me to MRI and high field magnetism. Most radiology residents hated the physics of MRI and were terrified of that section on the Boards. I sucked that stuff up!"

Jake noticed interest, so he continued. "But Dad wanted me to take over as CEO and President of Aerospace Consultants of Boston. His company controlled 3 billion dollars worth of government contracts."

"Sounds like you were on the right track, Jake. Where did you fuck up?" asked Susan, a glimmer of interest in her voice. It was a slight inflection that pulled her out of her usual character. She had never met anyone worth that much money. Frankly, it sounded like Daddy would probably be a better target, but you drink at the well closest to you.

"Well, when Dad got rid of me from home and set me up in an apartment on Beacon Hill, he also ended up getting rid of Mom. I never did get over the divorce. My new 'Mom' was about five years older than I was. My father and I started drifting even before that. When he found out I applied to Harvard Med, he called me a moron—told me that he spent his life setting me up in his billion-dollar company. Told me I would spend the rest of my life sticking my finger up people's assholes. I think my exact words were—'It takes one to know one, at least I wait until they get their periods before I fuck them.'

"I really think Dad would have taken it better if debutante teenage Mom wasn't in front of me when I said it."

"Good move, Einstein!" said Susan, smirk on her face.

"The rest is history. By the time I drove from Marblehead to Beacon Hill, the doorman got the call and I was politely informed that the locks would be changed by Monday and I had the weekend to move out. Mom put me up for about six months, but the divorce was a two-year process and she couldn't give me much money. Harvard Med was waiting for the check, and the Newton army recruiter's office had the papers in my hand in 48 hours! That was the last time Mom and I really spent much time together. She died of breast cancer 18 months ago. Dad didn't even come to the funeral."

"Sorry, Jake. Have you talked to your father since?"

"He tried to call me after I graduated from Harvard Med. I told him we could meet in front of Mom's grave. Guess he got the hint!"

Susan thought about it. She understood, but all of those millions—

"Time heals all wounds," she said with a sense of sadness. She gently touched his arm. "Maybe we can get a drink after we both get off-shift?"

"Yeah, that may be nice," whispered Jake. Deep inside he was grinning ear to ear. That line about his mother and breast cancer gets them every time! He had spoken with Mom yesterday. Most of the story was true, but after two years and four lawyers, she got 13 million and the estate at Martha's Vineyard. She took some art courses at Tufts and actually painted quite well. She wanted Jake at her first major showing at the Copley Place Art Gallery. Round two—Jake!

Tesla 6 was in the sub-basement of Walter Reed. The old bomb shelter was an ideal place for the most powerful magnet in the world. It actually occupied the old presidential suite.

Six inches of lead surrounded by four feet of concrete. The setup was a natural magnetic shield. The fact that it could withstand a 60-megaton nuclear warhead blast with DC as ground zero always gave a snicker to Colonel Sam Smith, Chief of Radiology and the T-6 project coordinator.

The security doors to the T-6 project opened with a four-note chime. The magnet was placed behind a paramagnetic screen of 18-karat gold mesh. The magnet was a behemoth structure made of four claws, closing on a central hollow bore with a gap just large enough to fit a 350- to 400-pound individual, causing moderate claustrophobia. The control room was a scene from NASA. Three consoles, digital timers, safety alarms, an airport metal detector tuned up about five hundred percent and located at the scanner entry door, and not much room for anything else. Lieutenant Susan Carlson was behind the control console and Smith was the radiologist of the day. General Paul Kovalik usually never came down to T-6. "If God had wanted us to fuck around with that much magnetism, he would have made us into refrigerators," Kovalik would say to Smith.

"Good morning, Paul," said Smith with his usual ass-kissing smile. "What brings you to the bowels of Walter Reed?"

"Sam, every once in a while the CO needs to get down there with the grunts," smiled Kovalik. He loved to kid Sam. Sam was never really the right stuff and Kovalik never liked ass-kissers, but after 5 years of knowing each other, this relationship was stable if not congenial. Sam was okay by Kovalik.

Susan was the duty tech and was wearing a non-magnetic paper gown especially designed for T-6 patients. The military never thought of designing gowns for technologists, so the gowns were typical hospital-design rear-closing patient gowns. Kovalik noticed how nicely it fit Susan, especially when she warmly saluted, "Good morning, General, sir!"

"Good morning, Lieutenant," responded Kovalik with the best poker face he could muster. He immediately turned to Smith.

"How is our T-6 project going? We talked about getting some NIH grant money. Any progress on your grant proposal?" asked Kovalik. He really knew the answer. Smith was never one to delve into the world of academia, and Kovalik wanted to finance at least two years of research before FDA approval of the magnet. This was his chance, and he knew Smith could not get him there.

"Well, Paul, you see, my pulse sequences are in the early evaluation phase. I don't want to push the envelope on this magnet. Nobody has ever used anything even close to it," stated Smith with a little discomfort in his voice.

"What do you think of Captain Eriksson? Seems like he did some decent research under Hahn on the GE T3 magnet at Mass General. His articles are quoted every month in *Radiology* and *AJR*. We may have a racehorse here, Sam," said Kovalik with just a little more force than Sam appreciated.

"I read Eriksson's proposal. Tumor shrinkage and increased tumor detectability at 3 Tesla with possible improved results at 6 Tesla. There is no convincing evidence in his preliminary data. A few case reports does not a paper make," said Smith. He clearly felt threatened by Jake.

"Eriksson was on the verge of getting a 2-million-dollar NIH grant which eventually went to Hahn, Sam. I agree, he is an arrogant bastard, but we need the funding. He sent me the proposal last week—" Kovalik could not finish the sentence before Smith's outburst.

"You see what I mean, I'm the Chief of Radiology. Eriksson had no authority to go over my head and send you the proposal after I rejected it!"

"Sorry, Smitty. I called Hahn yesterday for a reference. He told me Eriksson had his faults—mainly due to hound dog tendencies—but he was the most brilliant fellow they ever had at Harvard. I'm going to outrank you on this, buddy. He gets limited access to the magnet, five patients, and no slack in his usual assignments. I looked at your utilization charts, Sam. Nobody uses T-6 between midnight and 0600 hours. Let's see what the Wunderkind is made of," insisted Kovalik. It was a clear and direct order, not a recommendation.

"Under protest, Paul," answered Smith with most of the wind blown out of his sails.

"So noted," responded Kovalik. The privilege of command always gave him a sort of decadent rush. In Walter Reed, he was king, and to quote Mel Brooks, "It's good to be king!"

Susan listened attentively to the conversation. Her decision to have that drink with Jake last night—and coffee the following morning—again told her that her instincts were as sharp as ever. "Always bet on the winning racehorse," she whispered to herself.

Jake was coming on shift in the regular MRI suite of Walter Reed at about the same time his fate was being decided in the sub-basement. Rodriguez greeted him with his usual smile. "Did the mantis survive the evening, Captain?" he asked.

"Manny, the mantis survived not only the evening but went back for some morning prayer," smiled Jake.

"Please, Captain, please—please tell me you didn't use your dying mother and breast cancer sensitivity routine. I thought that was cruel and inhuman when you used that on Debbie in Pathology."

Jake smiled. "Well, in this version, Mom was already dead of breast cancer, but what's a little technicality? Susan was touched!"

"One of these days one of your lady friends is going to call your mother, and then don't expect me to come to the rescue. Anyway, Captain, looks like your head is still attached. I can't vouch for any other body parts, though," laughed Rodriguez.

"Actually, after yesterday's screw-up, I don't think I'll ever get on the T-6 project. Susan is just a diversion."

Jake no sooner finished his sentence than Kovalik entered the upstairs MRI suite. Both Jake and Rodriguez jumped to attention. Two visits from the hospital CO in just as many days. That could never be good news!

"At ease, at ease," mumbled Kovalik. "Eriksson, I want to see you in my office in thirty minutes."

"Sir," saluted Jake. He feared the worst. "Cleaning toilets in the DC Veterans Administration Hospital" were Kovalik's exact words—Shit!

Kovalik's office was well appointed, worthy of the Commanding Officer of Walter Reed and the personal physician of the President of the United States. On the wall, a series of diplomas, certificates, and medals. Hanging centrally on the wall, however, was Kovalik's most proud possession. Two photographs, blown up to 11 × 14. On the left, two soldiers in full Ranger gear, hands on each other's shoulders, jungle foliage behind them. It looked like Vietnam. The adjacent picture bore the Presidential seal. It was a golf shot taken at the Congressional Country Club of President David Sumner and General Paul Kovalik, hands on each other's shoulders. The thirty years that had passed were apparent, but their expressions were identical.

"At ease, Eriksson, you look a little green. I want to talk to you about the T-6 project," said Kovalik with forceful authority.

"Sir?" responded Jake,

"Smith and I talked about your research and I decided to give you some time on the magnet—"

"Thank you, sir!" said Jake emphatically. "I'll get through the twenty patients in my grant proposal in about two months. I can get Captain Jackson to cover me—"

"Eriksson!" shouted Kovalik. "I'm thrilled by your enthusiasm, but you didn't let me finish my sentence. You get five patients, between midnight and 0600 hours. We can't afford to cover your regular assignments. The only way I can allow this within our budget is if you cover your own shifts and do this on your own time, after hours. I want a personal written report after each patient or your research privileges are immediately revoked. Understood, Captain?"

"Yes, sir!" answered Jake with put-on bravado. "It is my privilege to work on the T-6 project in any capacity, sir!" Jake didn't quite understand Kovalik's change of heart, especially after their last interaction. But he wasn't about to ask any questions. He was about to break new ground and try his own experimental pulse sequences on the most powerful magnet in the world. Maybe his plans were coming together!

The T-6 suite at midnight was an eerie place. What Kovalik had failed to tell Jake was that even a technologist would be unavailable. Jake was the transport person, the orderly, and the technologist on his research project.

It really didn't matter. As long as he got magnet time! Jake started the pre-scan programming and RF warm-up sequence. The magnet was of the liquid-cooled superconductive type. A permanent magnet could not even come close to generating a 6 Tesla-magnetic field.

The T-6 was a special magnet with an electromagnetic core surrounded by an external liquid flux of electrons circulating at nearly the speed of light. It was housed within a liquid nitrogen absolute zero environment. The field was at 3 Tesla until the magnetic flux rings came out of the walls with a deep baritone rumble. An enormous doughnut-shaped ring would come out of the wall and encase the MRI central core, studded by microchip red LED lights flashing in a circle indicating magnet activation from 3 Tesla to 6 Tesla, a 30-second process. The supercooled liquid nitrogen was infused by a pump, providing a rhythmic backdrop—DUNGA! DUNGA! DUNGA!

Jake turned the T-6 on and left to get his patient. He saluted the armed security guard stationed outside of T-6. The guard's nickname was the Terminator. He had standing orders to shoot anyone breaching security. The joke was "T-2 guarding T-6."

Mrs. DeMarco was frail and frightened. Her skin was taught and yellow, a clear sign of jaundice associated with end-stage liver failure. It had been a long 8 months. From diagnosis to extensive metastatic disease, her breast cancer was not to be controlled by current medical technology. Sergeant DeMarco would not let her give up. General Paul Kovalik was a personal friend and told him Captain Jake Eriksson was the best. Paul Kovalik was always a straight shooter. He told him that Jinny didn't have much of a chance, but if there was any, this was it. Sergeant DeMarco, a tough, physically fit retired Master Sergeant, was with his wife every moment and accompanied her to the T-6 suite that evening.

"Mrs. DeMarco, Sergeant DeMarco, I have to go through the formality of obtaining an informed consent," started Jake.

"Don't bother, Captain, Jinny and I are in this together and know the score. General Kovalik personally told us about you and this magnet. Let's just get it over with."

"Tommy, I don't understand why I have to get into this paper gown. The MRI looks different than the other ones I had. I'm scared, Tommy, I'm scared!" cried Mrs. DeMarco.

"Jinny, it'll be all right, baby—we'll get this done just in time to watch the Friday night fights on ESPN," responded Sergeant DeMarco, turning to Jake. "I was all-division boxing champion in 1962. I'm still in great shape—work out every day. Jinny never liked to watch the fights, but after 40 years of marriage, she still tolerates me. I'm not changing anything in her last days!"

Putting Mrs. DeMarco in the claw-like magnet was a chore. Once it was closed, she would be even more claustrophobic. Even getting her on the stretcher was problematic.

"I want out, Tommy!" shouted Mrs. DeMarco, "I can't stand it—I'm afraid!"

"Can't I be in there with her?" asked Sergeant DeMarco. "I saw a TV show where the parents of a sick kid were at the foot of the stretcher when their kid got an MRI."

"Sergeant DeMarco, this magnet is a little different. You have to wear a special paper gown because your clothing has trace metal, and that could be dangerous. It is six times stronger than the magnets you've seen, and the magnetic field even ten feet around the magnet is as strong as inside the magnet. That's just the way magnetism works, and we can't rewrite physics." The DeMarcos' response told him that he better think rapidly—they were about to bail out!

"On the other hand," said Jake, "if we get you in a paper gown, you can hold your wife's leg, which will protrude slightly out of the magnet. We have done that for parents in the upstairs magnet. I'm still probably going to get into trouble for this, but hey—"

"Let's just get on with it! I'll get into the room with her. General Kovalik will understand. I've saved his ass a few times."

Sergeant DeMarco's touch immediately relaxed Mrs. DeMarco, despite the clanging of the RF coils in the magnet. He held her right ankle tightly. He was sitting on a non-magnetic plastic chair adjacent to the foot of the MRI stretcher. Jake was outside the magnet programming the console.

"Mrs. DeMarco, we are going to start with a 30-second pre-scan. You will hear some banging, then rapid clanging, and then a pause." He was able to see Sergeant DeMarco wave through the transparent gold anti-magnetic wire mesh.

The pre-scan completed exactly on time. The digital count-down timer was a bright red LED to the right of the computer screen. As the images scrolled onto the screen, Jake's pre-scan images showed much more than could be seen on the upstairs MRI. Mrs. DeMarco had virtually no normal liver left!

Although his prior research had been performed on rats only, the Hahn/Eriksson (as it had become known in the radiographic literature) STIR pulse sequence resulted not only improved visualization, but 30 percent tumor reduction in end-stage cancer. At 6 Tesla, the magnetic field effects may cause even greater tumor regression. STIR was an acronym for Short Tao Inversion Recovery. Eriksson invented it using quantum physics equations he derived during his engineering years at MIT. The answer, however, was a 20-minute pulse sequence away.

"Mrs. DeMarco, we are going to start the final sequence now. The noise will be a little different, but don't worry, your husband will squeeze your ankle to tell you everything is OK."

Jake's comment was acknowledged by a thumbs-up from Sergeant DeMarco, who was gently rubbing and squeezing his wife's ankle.

Jake programmed the first 6 Tesla scan using his experimental STIR sequence. The elapsed time LED display was at 0 hrs, 0 min. The pulse sequence countdown timer was at 20 min, 0 sec. The machine was set on manual override since the Hahn/Eriksson STIR pulse sequence was not accepted by the computer as a "safe or approved" sequence and could only be activated and stopped manually.

Jake had a hard time concentrating. He had been on call last night, on Susan the night before, and on experimental duty tonight. Nonetheless, women, research, and career always came before sleep—in that order.

"Here we go!" announced Jake as he manually activated the 20-minute pulse sequence.

That was the last thing he remembered.

The shrill beeping of the overheat warning alarm awoke Jake out of a sound sleep. His head was resting on the MRI console. His neck hurt from the unusual position of his slumber. After a few seconds of disorientation, his response was panic.

"Oh, my god!" cried Jake, staring at the elapsed time indicator. "She's been in there for two hours and seventeen minutes!"

His first glance was at the EKG monitor above the console. Mrs. DeMarco had a leaking mitral valve and her heart would probably be the first to go.

He was relieved. The EKG was in normal sinus rhythm. Jake's horror, however, would start when he looked into the scanner through the gold mesh. Sergeant DeMarco was face down on his wife's leg, leaning unnaturally against the MRI stretcher. Jake, gowned in paper, ran inside the magnet and firmly shook Sergeant DeMarco's shoulder. The sergeant's lifeless body fell on the floor like a sack of potatoes!

"Shit, this can't be happening!" yelled Jake. He immediately checked for respiration and a carotid pulse. There was none! Sergeant DeMarco was cool to the touch. He had been dead for some time. Jake had no options. He ran outside the magnetic field and into the control room, pushed the wall intercom button, and shouted "Code Blue, Tesla 6 Magnet Suite, sub-basement—repeat, Code Blue, Tesla 6, sub-basement!"

Jake then dragged the body out of the magnetic room so that the code team could do their work. They arrived within 45 seconds, but Jake knew they were just going through the motions. He let the team run the code while he pulled Mrs. DeMarco out of the scanner. He wanted her out of the area.

Jake activated the manual open sequence and the giant claws of the magnetic tunnel opened, fully retracting the superconducting doughnut and opening the central gantry. Mrs. DeMarco appeared confused but in no acute distress. It was late and Jake was in his own Twilight Zone, but something about her bothered him. He did not know what. This was no time to think but a time to act. "Mrs. DeMarco, we are going to get you out of here and back to your room, okay?"

Mrs. DeMarco's stare was empty, a look of no understanding. It didn't matter; he had to get her out. She stared without any emotion at the code team doing chest compression and ambo bag breathing on the sergeant as they quickly passed into the hallway. Jake could not imagine what she was feeling.

By the time Jake returned to the T-6 suite, he saw a covered body being rolled out of the control room. The code team leader was a surgical resident named Milosovich, a no-bullshit guy. Jake had been out drinking with him a few times.

"Hey, Jakey, what the hell happened in there? I always told you that you should consider leaving radiology and becoming a real doctor!" laughed Milosovich. "On the other hand, I say scan them before they die! That way the insurance companies pay better. That guy looked like he was on his last pint of blood, pale and jaundiced as hell!"

It was the typical gallows humor doctors used to minimize the personal emotional damage of their work. It was hard looking death in the eye. Such humor sounded callous but it helped them survive reality.

"Yeah," answered Jake absently, looking at Mrs. DeMarco's repeat STIR liver scan on the MRI monitor. The MRI showed an entirely normal liver! How?

2

REVEREND MORTEN DUBLAISE

THE BROWN BOX delivered to the back delivery bay of the NIH had the usual UPS markings. The usual UPS truck delivered it. NIH security was moderately tight, but the National Institutes of Health in Bethesda averaged 750 packages a day. Only packages labeled "Biochemical Hazard" got attention.

Considering the pathogens they received from around the world, the mailroom at the NIH was something akin to a Level 4 Quarantine Unit. One mistake and the greater Washington DC area would be at risk.

It happened in 1994 with an unusual strain of Ethiopian primate Ebola virus. The container ruptured and a 100-block radius was quarantined. The press never got wind of the real problem and the evacuation was attributed to a broken gas pipe, but four NIH directors were immediately terminated.

This special package was labeled "X-RAY FILM, DO NOT EXPOSE TO RADIATION OR LIGHT." This immediately triggered the bypass sequence initiated by the Radiology Department and the Genetic Chromatography Division. The last time X-ray film went through the usual airport security unit at the NIH, about $40,000 worth of film was destroyed.

The running joke was "I never believed the security guards at the airport who told me to leave my camera in the bag, the film won't be damaged." All NIH employees who knew that story took cameras out when they entered airport terminals.

The mailroom clerk delivered the box personally to the office of Dr. Jacoby, Genetic Engineering and Cloning Division, NIH. At exactly 2:35 pm, the 20 pounds of French plastic explosive detonated, destroying the entire West Wing of the NIH. The wing housed some of the most prominent biochemical and genetic researchers in the world. Reverend Morten Dublaise knew that. He knew the layout, the delivery schedule, the doctor's schedule; he knew everything.

Reverend Morten Dublaise's long, dark career started with his years as an enigmatic minister of the Southern Baptist Church, moving from small Southern parish to small Southern parish every two to three years. He stood five feet, nine inches tall but looked significantly taller. His eyes were a piercing ice-blue, his voice soft but passionate. He always wore a priest's collar, developing the habit of rubbing the inside of his collar with the forefinger of his right hand. Sometimes the children of his parish would make fun and imitate this tic.

As a child, he remembered the shock on his teacher's faces when they received his IQ scores back in his junior year in high school. He graduated from State University with a double major, Religious Studies and Clinical Psychology. Morten had a brilliant mind, but he never behaved or excelled like someone with an IQ of 184. He thought of different things and he never had anything in common with the other students. He never dated.

Morten loved his study of psychology. To him, religion was its application! Like any good mechanic, he appreciated learning to use new tools. His were the tools of the mind. The minds of others were something for him to mold.

He started slowly, watching influential teachers and their mannerisms. Morten had the uncanny ability to change his vocal patterns and inflections dynamically. It was as if he could feel the tenor of his audience. He was capable of being everything to everybody. If twenty people were asked to give a descriptor of the good Reverend, the inquisitor would probably get twenty personality profiles.

As he aged, he became even more reclusive and demure in appearance, but as a minister his sermons were piercing. "He could make a Jew go to church," said many of his parishioners. Dublaise could do more than that!

The Reverend had lived nearly two years in Little Knox, Tennessee, when his urges started again. He promised himself that he would not succumb to the temptations of the flesh, but his calling was strong and the Lord spoke to him often.

"Let thy way be the way of purity. Let not temptation crawl into your breast, for as I resisted the carnal flesh, so shall you, my Messiah! Temptation is evil and the harbinger of temptation is the avatar of the devil. So shall you be my avatar. So shall you destroy temptation where it stands!"

Linda Stanfield was the usual flirtatious 18-year-old. She had just graduated from high school, and her debutante days were over. It was time for a job, marriage, and babies. She volunteered at the church Tuesdays and Sundays, helping out with the paperwork, church activities, and cleanup. Many thought Linda wore blouses that were a little too low. She made up for that by wearing skirts that were a little too high. A girl has to have a little fun!

She thought Reverend Dublaise was a nice man but always felt uncomfortable under his gaze, something she never experienced with the other ministers. His sermons, however, were so passionate and so full of fire and brimstone she doubted that he had a lustful bone in his body. Unfortunately, she was very wrong.

He stared at her every week, noticing the shape of her buttocks as she seductively bent over. Sometimes, getting just a glimpse of her round, full breasts exposed ever so slightly over her blouse. Her smile was that of a temptress, her lips inviting.

The Lord had warned him of her powers. It was not his fault. Most saints had their temptations. The Lord taught them how to free their spirits of sin and liberate the vehicles of temptation. It was never easy. Doing the Lord's work is never easy.

She was to be Dublaise's next target. She was but a vehicle of the Devil, a vessel designed as a harbinger of his destruction. She was his test—Again!

"Why did the Lord have to test him so often?" he wondered.

As their time together passed, her humanity disappeared. In the eyes of Dublaise, only evil and temptation remained. That was how it always started. He never saw himself as a murderer, but as an extension of the hand of the Lord. He did nothing of his own will, but only as commanded.

"This child is not what she seems, Morten," spoke the holy apparition. "She is an incarnation of the Devil. You have tried to teach her my ways. Your sermons were just, but your arrow missed its mark. As Abraham was asked to sacrifice his own son, I shall ask you to sacrifice one of your flock. The path of the righteous is never easy. The path of the Messiah is even harder."

Reverend Dublaise had heard this message before. He had no choice but to follow the way of the Lord. He had to destroy this evil incarnation before its lustful allure destroyed him.

On a cold November evening, Linda was just finishing her paperwork in the small office behind the altar when a creak in the wooden floor startled her. "Reverend Dublaise, you scared the living daylights out of me!" cried Linda, hands clutching her chest, respiration rapid.

"I'm sorry, my child, I saw the light and didn't realize you were working so late. I thought you had left hours ago," responded Dublaise.

"Actually, I had a date with Bobby, but at the last minute he decided to go drinking with his friends at Jeffersonville College. He asked me to drive up with him, but those boys are pigs, if you know what I mean, Reverend. I figured Mom and Dad weren't expecting me home until later anyway, so I might as well catch up on some of these church bills."

Linda was wearing jeans with a tightly fitting V-neck sweater. Dublaise heard every word she said but could only concentrate on Linda's lovely young body. His inner urges were erupting in a satanic fervor. His brow and upper lip were sweating feverishly.

His moment had come, as it had come many times before. As Mary Magdalene tested Christ, he was being tested. He approached her with a blank stare. Linda had already gotten out of her chair, frightened by the creaking of the floorboards, and was leaning on the front ledge of the large oak desk, facing Dublaise.

"Are you okay?" asked Linda with a definite quiver in her voice.

Dublaise remained silent but continued to approach. He could smell Linda's sweet lilac perfume, almost taste her lips. He slowly lifted his left hand and touched her breast—an uncontrollable urge possessed his body. His intoxication was ephemeral as Linda started screaming and pushing. He did not hear a single sound. Dublaise was possessed by passion, by anger, by that feeling he had often had in the past.

We all know the way, we walk the path, but then someone hands us an irresistible bribe. A flower blooming in the desert. A temptation so irresistible that only the true believer can even hope to escape.

"What are you doing, Reverend—my God—get away—leave me alone!" screamed Linda. She did not understand.

The Reverend's next move was almost instinctive, grabbing the stem of a heavily weighted brass lamp at the edge of the desk and smashing it into Linda's skull. The large gash started pulsating bright red blood as the blow transected her temporal artery. But Linda was young, and other than in the movies, people rarely died from one blow.

The harder Linda fought, the harder Dublaise bludgeoned her. Even after she stopped fighting back, he continued to smash her in the head and face, as if each and every blow served to further purify his soul.

Once his holy sacrifice was over, he lay on the floor next to Linda's body for hours, caressing her lifeless flesh, first sobbing, but then overcome by a feeling of sanctification and elation. His purity had returned. He did his job with alacrity and swiftness.

"It's always the same, Lord," he murmured. "They tempt us but we win in the end. It's always the same."

The next series of events was well rehearsed. It was repeated in every town where Dublaise had a parish. Dublaise knew what needed to be done.

He dragged the body into the basement and placed it next to the wall plug he used in the church tool shop. He then returned upstairs to the kitchen pantry and found the electric turkey carver. Dublaise placed the carver by the door, went to the desk Linda had been, working at, and found her purse. He was looking for her car keys. Finding them, he went outside and put the car into the church barn.

Dublaise returned to the basement with lawn bags in hand. He plugged the knife into the wall and slowly started dismembering her. He remembered seeing such scenes in silly movies. In real life, there was no squirting or pulsating blood. Lividity had set in, and the only blood was a slow ooze onto the lawn bags scattered on the basement floor.

Removing the head was always the part he hated, especially that involuntary opening of the eyes that always occurred when the cervical spine was separated from the thoracic spine. The head, however, was the most important part. That was where the dental records were kept, and he knew all of the forensic traps to avoid.

The dismemberment, the scattered burial along random country roads, and the cleanup were always followed by the Sheriff's questions:

"No, officer, she left here at around six o'clock, something about going with her boyfriend to Jeffersonville. That's the last time I saw her."

The usual investigation of course yielded nothing. Another pretty girl disappears in the South. Big city detectives or the FBI rarely got involved—too many larger fish to fry.

This time, however, a stranger came to town and was asking questions. He flashed an FBI badge. Nothing came of the inquiry, Dublaise was far too smart for that, but it was time to move on to a different parish.

It's hard to imagine whether certain pivotal events in history are coincidental or part of some great master plan. The coincidence theory makes you want to purchase a lottery ticket, whereas the master plan theory makes you want to go to your nearest house of worship. Regardless of theory, the arrival of Dublaise in Goshen, Montana, was a turning point in his life.

As things got hotter in Little Knox, Dublaise realized he needed to get out of the fire fast. The Baptist parish listings were few and most available ministries were in remote places where nobody wanted to live. Goshen had been without a priest for three years. The arid climate was a deterrent to even the most devout minister.

A parish close to the end of the world—perfect! When things quieted down, he would come back to the South, where he felt at home. Little did he know he was about to meet destiny—a match made in hell!

After his arrival, he realized why the parish was empty. Goshen and its surrounding towns were the center of a remote paramilitary group, the Children of Freedom. Approximately 500 God-fearing Christians armed to the teeth with automatic weapons, explosives, and even heavy artillery, ready to protect the American way—at all cost. Of course, that meant no blacks, Jews, government, taxes, or any authority. They were loosely organized, with no leadership. They had no firm beliefs other than deep-seated bigotry, hatred, and a maniacal suspicion of government authority. At their core lay a unified hatred of all technology and technological advancement. "The government and the scientists are meddling with nature. They're messing around with things only God should touch; genetic engineering, high technology, cloning, transplants, medical research. God sent AIDS to destroy the homosexuals. There should be no cure!" These were the shouts heard in their town meetings.

Morten Dublaise was home. He had found his flock and they had found the Messiah. The voices suddenly stopped for Dublaise. He no longer needed the guidance of the Lord, for the Lord sayeth: "Thou shalt recognize me when I again walk amongst my children, and thou shalt call me Jehovah!" He was Jehovah!

Within three years, Dublaise unified the Children of Freedom in his newly formed Church and gave them purpose and religious fervor where there had been none. He focused their hatred and lifted them above religion—and Christianity. The Ministry excommunicated him, but that mattered not. His charismatic personality erupted and followers responded to his messianic sermons. His powers of coercive mind control were enormous. He still wore his priest's collar, an image he found difficult to release. As always, his right forefinger continually rubbed the irritated area of his neck underneath the well-starched neckpiece.

He read and religiously studied Robert Jay Lifton's eight-point model of thought reform:

1. Environmental control
2. Mystical manipulation

3. Demand for purity
4. Cult of confession
5. Sacred science
6. Loaded language
7. Doctrine over person
8. Dispensing of existence

Lifton's original model, published and designed as a help-ful guide to detect cults and tactics of coercive persuasion, was brilliantly manipulated into the very tools Dublaise would use to entrap and control his followers. He understood the text as a model not of what to look out for, but rather of how to exert mind control tactics. The hunted became the hunter, using the very tools designed to trap him.

Paramilitary and religious groups from Wyoming, North Dakota, South Dakota, and Northern Idaho heard of the Messiah and his powers. By the time he made the FBI's Most Wanted list, the Army of the Messiah had 200,000 members at large. The inner sanctum remained in Goshen, where Dublaise was worshipped as the Messiah. His Apostles would set up Churches of Armageddon throughout the Midwest. Dublaise took personal pride in teaching the ways of the Messiah to his Apostles. The Eight Points were translated into *The Eight Religious Paths to Eternal Salvation*, written as a primer to be carried at all times. The "children" would be rewarded for completing each of the steps. Indoctrination was a one-way ticket. It was like the Roach Motel—you can check in, but you can never leave—ALIVE!

The document presented to the U.S. Supreme Court in 1996 as an educational Appendix on Coercive Psychological Systems: the case of *Sapperstein v. Church of the Sanctified 89-1367 and 89-1361* sparked government intervention in U.S. cult activity and started the FBI investigation of the Army of the Messiah. It cited Lifton's model for identification of brainwashing and cult activity and specifically referred to a copy of the Dublaise *Eight Paths to Eternal Salvation* as the most flagrant use of mind control tactics in modern history. The published exhibit had Lifton's model side by side with the Dublaise path. It elicited a chill in all readers of and participants in the hearing.

A special division of the FBI was instituted to study cults using coercive mind control tactics. The Dublaise cult was their number one target. They were thought dangerous not only because of cult activity, but because of the paramilitary anti-government nature of their preachings. Religious wackos were one thing. Armed religious wackos preaching the end of the world were another. The cult was spreading like wildfire.

The FBI started with a background check on Dublaise's life. Parish by parish, the story started to fit. There was death at every turn. Quiet, well-disguised, but death! Then came the more recent family complaints about missing relatives. Relatives who had left the Army of the Messiah only to mysteriously disappear soon after being reunited with their families. Two years after the start of the investigation, bodies started to be discovered. Decomposed female body parts near Dublaise's parishes in the South. Two mass graves in Montana, one in South Dakota, all containing the bodies of escaped cult members—"Roach Motel."

The mass graves were found with the help of informants. Protective custody was the guarantee. Jurisdictions were argued, but a Montana trial was denied. The trial of the decade was to be held in Fairfax, County Federal Court, Fairfax, Virginia, the location of one of Reverend Dublaise's early female victims.

3
PHU HUA DONG, VIETNAM

1967 WAS A shit year for Paul Kovalik. He was 23 years old, the son of a Polish foundry worker in Pittsburgh. Paul was just getting on the right track—then he got his draft notice. It was the middle of the Vietnam "conflict." That always sounded like something akin to a bar brawl—unless you were unlucky enough to ship out.

He remembered that fateful week as if it was yesterday, but then again, in his memory, it almost was. It was the start of his rollercoaster ride.

On Friday, July 13, he received his letter from the Armed Forces Medical Center, Bethesda, Maryland:

> Dear Lieutenant Kovalik,
>
> Your application to the Armed Forces School of Medicine has been approved pending satisfactory completion of your final year at The State College of Pennsylvania. Your military scholarship will require two years of military service for each year of your medical education in addition to the time owed for your college tuition sponsorship.

It was the best day in his life. The first Kovalik to become a doctor! No more stupid Polish jokes.

On Monday, July 16, the second letter came. Only two days later. It was simple form notice:

To: Lieutenant Paul Kovalik, notice of service activation;
report to Charleston AFB, South Carolina 0900 August 1,
1967 for immediate deployment to Jungle Operations Training
Center, Panama City, Panama.

It had to be a mistake! They needed doctors more than 2nd
Lieutenants. A few phone calls was all it would take. Then
again, he always had a feeling that his prior Army Ranger
training would nail him into active combat duty.

"Selective Service Detailer's Office, Draft Bureau of Personnel," answered a terse female voice.

"Hello, may I please speak with Colonel Weston?" asked
Paul. It took him about 30 calls to just get the inside telephone
number of Weston.

"Weston here!" answered an even more terse voice.

As the Bureau of Personnel CO, Weston heard every
bullshit story known to man. He had every local government
official, senator, and even presidential aide calling him for
favors. All East Coast duty assignments went through the
Detailer's office, and he was Commanding Officer.

Paul started talking very slowly. He was calculating, forceful, and yet respectful.

"Sir, this is 2nd Lieutenant Paul Kovalik, Army Ranger
Unit Reserve. I believe that you have my records."

Paul made enough phone calls and pulled enough strings
to get his records to Weston—sometimes that works for you in
the military. This time, however, the call that Weston received
asking to pull Kovalik's records was made by Colonel Wyatt
from Fort Bragg. Weston thought Wyatt was an asshole. Paul
had no idea that the decision on his fate was already made
based on just that simple fact.

"Lieutenant Kovalik, I am a busy man so I won't waste
your time or mine. Your Ranger record is exemplary. We need
platoon leaders more than we need Park Avenue Doctors paid
by the military. Because of your record, I pulled some strings.
Your place in medical school has been held for you for the

class of 1969. Good luck, son, I'm sure you will make your country proud."

For a Ranger, Jungle Training School was easy. Panama City was a nice place to get drunk every night. The daily jaunts into the rain forest were supposed to be prep for Vietnam.

Close, but no cigar. The rain was torrential, it was muggy, they scaled mountains, crossed swamps, waded through rivers filled with leeches, parasites, and things not even catalogued in books, but there was one difference. Nobody was trying to blow your head off.

Special Operations, or SpecOps, from every military service trained at Fort Sherman in Panama City. You make some friends and then ship out. Some you may see again. Many will never come back. That makes it easy to bond. These men were the elite and there were a lot of "good guys."

You can spot a good guy immediately. You drink together, go on maneuvers, save each other's asses when the CO asks questions that you don't want answered. Then you get a nickname that sticks with you for the rest of your life. For Paul, it was easy. He was pre-med, going to medical school after the war—he could only be called one thing—"Doc."

Doc met Indian for the first time at Melinda's, a salty bar on the Atlantic part of town in Panama City. The place was a shithole frequented by mainly military and of course, the requisite women engaged in the oldest of professions.

The bar smelled like stale beer, the floor was made of warped wood planking with a smattering of sawdust, presumably to soak up spilled beer and puke. It didn't matter. This was a wartime soldier's bar, and cold beer was the only requirement.

SpecOps forces always gravitated in their own little groups. Navy Seals hung out in the back corner, the Berets in the front next to the juke box, the Aussie Special Forces at the bar (of course), and the Rangers right next to the bathroom.

The Rangers figured it was the most strategic place in the bar since the beer flowed in as easily as it flowed out. They got to check everybody out and they never even had to get up. Tonight was no different.

Doc got there at around 2230 hours. Ranger Team B was already into their third round of brew when Doc sat next to Indian.

Indian was Team B's platoon leader, a big Ivy League-type guy named David Sumner. His clean presence set some of the grunts off, until Indian loosened them up. He was a born leader. It was as if he could read minds. He was able to adjust to any environment. With grunts, he cursed and downed beers like a sewer rat. Among officers, his West Point training was eminently noticeable. But most importantly, he led by example—usually with an incredible right hook that came out of nowhere.

They called him Indian because he was All-American in lacrosse. Right after the Point, he joined the Rangers and a grunt mockingly asked him what the fuck lacrosse was.

"Lacrosse," said Sumner, "is the toughest fuckin' game on earth, where we take sticks with small nets attached and beat the shit out of each other with almost no equipment or rules. We take a ball harder than your head and try to ram it into a net defended by some poor bastard who feels like target practice. It was invented by American Indians, who, rumor has it, used the shrunken heads of their enemies for balls, but your head would probably be too ugly even for them to use—any other questions, asshole?"

He was called Indian from then on. No more questions!

Indian became kind of a legend in Jungle Training School. He brought Team B in first on every operation. Doc was glad to finally meet him and they immediately hit it off, although Paul came from the other side of the tracks. David's father was a state senator, but they both approached life with brains and brawn, a rarity in the military.

They were pretty plowed when an over-the-hill hooker came over to the Ranger table.

"Any of you gentleman interested in buying a lonely virgin a drink?" asked the lady, who still had a subtle glint in her eye. She had a body that looked better after the sixth round of beer.

One of the Aussies at the bar noticed the come-on and shouted, "Look at the Rangers, mates! I 'ear they teach 'em to fock pigs instead of eatin' thim in their trainin'." The resultant laughter from the Australians at the bar was raucous.

Doc was never known for controlling his temper. Having four military units in close proximity was always a setup for a fight. Add beer, soldiers from different countries throwing insults, and an undeniable lady's honor at stake, and what you get is a spark on gasoline.

Doc connected with a right hook and the lead Aussie's nose would never again be centrally located on his face. Blood gushed out of it uncontrollably.

Unfortunately, this placed Doc in the middle of the bar surrounded by four pissed Australian trained killers. The Aussies always prided themselves on their unarmed combat techniques, and Doc had a feeling that protecting this lady's honor may have not been worth it—then again, they had insulted the Rangers!

Before Doc could react to protect himself, he saw Indian lunge sideways, across two of the Aussies, throwing them off balance. Doc instinctively ducked and rammed his fist into the third oncoming soldier's gut. Indian then finished up the two Aussies he flew across within seconds. One right elbow to the ear and a left knee to the groin.

"Hey, Indian!" shouted Doc. "For a West Pointer, you sure fight dirty!"

"Doc, you learn to hit them where they hurt—an old lacrosse trick. The other lacrosse trick is to do it and not get caught. Let's get the fuck outta here!"

The other advantage to being near the bathroom is obvious to any Ranger worth his salt—the bathroom is always near the back door! They both lunged out seconds before the MPs arrived.

The next morning was a little rough. The CO announced that there was some trouble in town and that Rangers were rumored to be involved in unfriendly interactions with their Australian "comrades." As a sign of good faith, Team A and B were "asked" to march double time for 20 miles with full gear.

Doc and Indian glanced at each other and subtly smiled. It was worth it! They had beaten the shit out of those arrogant Aussies. If they didn't know better, it almost seemed as if the CO also had a smirk on his face.

The following week was their last week in Panama. Everyone shipped out to their assignments. Doc had a week to get to Travis AFB in California and then Nam. Indian got the same assignment. Two Ranger teams were sent in to refresh the 1st Infantry Division at Long Binh. They were both to report to the 90th Replacement Battalion for further orders.

Indian's orders specified a promotion to 1st Lieutenant with deployment to Rear Echelon Main Force, Bien Hoa Air Force Base. "Mr. U.S. Senator Dad" had a lot to say about his son's deployment.

Rear Echelon or REMFs was polite society lingo. The Rangers called them "Rear Echelon Mother Fuckers." No action, lotta Vietnamese pussy, and the requisite Distinguished Medal Award.

Doc had no such pull. When his deployment orders were posted on the bulletin board at Bien Hoa, they read reassignment, 5th Infantry Division, Phu Cong/Shau Valley. His reassignment was not uncommon. Assignments in Nam, however, were predictors. Within hours of landing and deployment, the boys knew the scoop. An assignment up north was tantamount to a death sentence—the Shau Valley was up north.

Doc's first days at Phu Cong were confusing at best. His CO gave him command of Company C and an immediate field promotion to First Louie. It felt good initially—until the platoon CO told him that the last 1st Lieutenant nearly wiped out his company by leading them into an anti-personnel mine field. The guy's mom and dad got his dog tags—and some intestinal contents.

Suffice it to say, his stateside funeral was a closed-casket event. Doc was smart enough to know the score—a 2nd Louie is dog meat, a 1st Louie is not much better, and the only way to lead a company is from the front, with your sergeant at your side. This was no war game, and Doc knew it. So did Sergeant Moulder.

Moulder was an enlisted man from Johnstown, Pennsylvania. They called him "Duster" because his whole family worked in the coal mines of Pennsylvania. Rumor, however, had it that his nickname, had something to do with an incident in Lai Khe where a green 2nd Louie was about to lead the platoon into an obvious ambush. Duster knew the score but the Lieutenant wouldn't listen.

Lieutenant Lake was an arrogant college grad who thought war was something like a scene from Gone with the Wind. Close, but Cecil B. DeMille was not on the set, and a bunch of soldiers with no experience were about to die.

Anyway, nobody knows where the sniper bullet came from—then again, Duster got his platoon out with only one casualty, Lieutenant Lake.

Doc was not about to make the same mistake. Rumors about friendly fire were true, and the Special Ops forces Doc trained under were leaders trained to look for morale problems.

Duster also immediately sensed Doc's roots, and they both knew and understood the score. Soon after, Charlie Company had the highest enemy body count in the battalion and the fewest casualties.

The attack orders came down Christmas, 1968. Three battalions were to engage a Viet Cong stronghold in the village of Phu Hua Dong (PHD). Charlie Company, led by Doc, was to divert the enemy by faking a southern recon mission, which would change at Highway 13 to a westward and eventually northward path leading them above the enemy at PHD.

Alpha Company would do the same but take the opposite eastern diversionary route. By 0550 hours, January 2, 1969, Alpha and Charlie Company were to simultaneously attack PHD from the north. At 0650 hours, Southern Division's Delta Company out of Lai Khe would launch a direct northerly offensive. The theory was that this unexpected series of attacks would flank the VC on three sides, making the ambush indefensible. Unless of course it was expected!

At 0550 hours, Doc gave the silent attack signal. They converged on Phu Hua Dong and secured the perimeter within 30 minutes. The village was, however, deserted. The soldiers looked at each other in turn. Nobody expected the silence. Only birds were heard fluttering in the distance.

Hut-by-hut recon was deadly and to be avoided at all cost, but they had no option. Alpha Company was nowhere in sight and they were in the middle of a deserted VC village. The quiet was deafening. An occasional crackle was heard from the kindling of smoldering cooking pits. The VC had been there recently. Duster came up to Doc with an uncharacteristic worried look.

"We're fucked, Doc! It's a trap—been there and done it!" They were the last words he would ever say. The sniper bullet hit Duster in the chest without even the slightest warning. Doc had seen chest wounds before and knew the verdict. Duster was dead before he ever hit the dusky Vietnamese soil. Doc had no time even to even respond to his fallen friend. Small arms fire erupted everywhere. The ambush they were planning was their own.

"Retreat into tight quarters, Hill 52!" shouted Doc. He fired randomly into the surrounding jungle while retreating to the northeast corner of the village, a fallback zone they called Hill 52. It was nothing more than a mound of dirt, but three sides could be protected. Doc watched as his men were slaughtered, one by one. They had no chance. They had been expected.

"Contact Alpha Company. Where the fuck are they? The east side of PHD is swarming with Viet Cong and we're outgunned 10 to 1. Get some fucking help!" screamed Doc to Radar, the communications officer. Radar was the only other soldier to make it to Hill 52 in one piece.

"Charlie Company, this is Central Command, do you copy?" shrieked a muffled voice.

"Copy—this is Charlie, encountering massive enemy resistance. Where is Alpha Company—break—requesting immediate support from Alpha Company!" cried Radar. The anguish could be heard in his voice.

"Alpha Company has been radio silent since 0300 hours, repeat—you are on your own!" The response was from a lifeless gray metallic box. The words had no meaning, no humanity. There was no person on the other side, just a mechanical voice saying, "You're fucked, soldier—it is now time to die for your country."

A barrage of AK-47 rifle fire accompanied the message. Doc was thinking of his alternatives. Most of his platoon was dead. Duster, his most trusted soldier, had a six-inch hole in his chest, his backup platoon was probably wiped out before they even got near the village, and he was stuck on a piss-ass hill called 52 with a nerd holding a radio as his main offensive weapon.

Their only hope was to last until Delta Company could come in from the south. Gallant shiny infantry to the rescue! Just like in the John Wayne movies. Then an AK-47 round blasted through the front of Radar's head.

The military medic lectures during training showed wound films depicting entry and exit wounds. Their goal was to desensitize soldiers to the horrors of war. They even showed closed-head damage where the bullet kind of bounces around in your cranial vault until your brain is a "vegematic" commercial—but reality was different. Somehow, it just doesn't resemble a training film. Radar had family back home. That part is hard to forget!

Although it sounds stupid, your response is always the same—"Radar! Radar! Come on, buddy, don't die on me, man! Who the fuck is going to tune in the baseball scores from the states?" But it really didn't matter. Doc knew.

The next sound he heard was a muffled thud—then another thud. He felt a twinge in his left chest and then a rabbit punch in his left flank. With his next deep breath he felt his lung expand, but he also heard the sucking sound of air entering the outside of his left chest.

Doc knew. He had an open chest wound with a tension pneumothorax. He looked to his right and saw Radar's lifeless body, leaning unnaturally on a rock. Brain tissue and skull fragments were splattered all over his chest. No matter—Doc needed a chest pack and he needed it now.

Using his hip knife, he tore Radar's shirt off in one quick motion. Doc knew that if he didn't seal the hole in his chest, his next breath would be his last. He adeptly wrapped Radar's soiled shirt and rammed it into the gaping wound. Doc knew enough to use his last breath to blow out every ounce of air from his lung, equilibrating the pressure inside and outside his chest. His next breath was easier. That was the good news. The bad news was his right flank. The second bullet had gone right through his flank and Doc could see right inside his abdomen. The brown stuff oozing out came from his colon. The pulsating bright red arterial blood was probably from of his kidney. He knew he was all but dead.

Using pieces of cloth from his own uniform as well as Radar's, Doc made a damn good compression field dressing. He really had no idea why, but the thought of dying without fighting until the bitter end never occurred to him. He was working on pure adrenaline and instinct.

After packing his flank wound, he listened to the small arms firing randomly scattered along the village. He felt good. His boys would fight until the end. It then came to him—he would fight until the end, too, and then blow some VC ass to kingdom come!

Doc slowly reached into his web gear and pulled out a grenade. With his left hand, he dislodged the pin and gently wedged it between the ground and his right shoulder blade. He would do his best to stay conscious. When the VC approached or picked him up, BOOM!

By now his blood loss was affecting his consciousness. He drifted in and out of a stupor. Fine by him—what better way to die than by blowing up and taking some VCs with you? Doc didn't remember much afterward. Artillery fire intensified and he was proud of his boys.

At 0325 hours southern Delta Squadron was making good progress towards the north. Phu Hua Dong was six clicks due northeast. Indian was platoon leader. He knew his job and resented Daddy pulling strings to place him in the southern REMFs.

If Dad could see him now! Laos was three clicks due west, North Vietnam seven clicks due north, and his platoon was heading into a region the Green Berets called the Devil's Asshole.

Then again, Indian was an Army Ranger—assholes were their specialty. He was tired of doing perimeter patrols around his CO's tent. About the only thing he protected the Army base from were incoming whores—not that they weren't tough or anything, but a punch in the nose usually did the trick. Besides, he knew volunteering for this assignment meant he got to see his buddy Doc in Charlie Company. They probably had some great stories to exchange.

One click from PHD, Sparky Delta Squadron's comm. officer got a priority one message. "HQ to Delta Squadron, HQ to Delta Squadron. Alpha and Charlie Companies down! Enemy forces massive. Casualties high. Mission scrubbed—REPEAT, MISSION SCRUBBED!"

Indian looked at Sergeant O'Malley with a look that left nothing to be said. O'Malley's brother was the comm. officer for Charlie Company. Indian was not about to let Doc down, regardless of odds.

That was what Nam was all about. Nothing mattered, not life, not death, not heroics. Just honor. Protecting your buddies because they protected your ass. The other bullshit only counted in boardrooms on Wall Street and Capitol Hill.

"O'Malley, these hills are really fucking up our radio reception, aren't they?" asked Indian.

"I can't make out shit, Lieutenant—how about you, Sparky?" asked O'Malley.

"I don't know, Sarge, this thing has been acting funny ever since we left HQ."

They hit Phu Hua Dong at dawn, expecting the worst. They got it. The VC didn't expect a southern hit. Indian ordered a forty-five-degree flanking maneuver and his two flanks opened fire on the village simultaneously. The VC was caught cleaning up the mess when they were hit with small and intermediate automatic weapons fire. Their intelligence obviously failed to detect the southern attack, and the ambush was over within 20 minutes.

The VC troops on the northern part of the village had their back door. The VC was never much for sustained combat. They preferred a hit-and-run strategy. Indian expected the exit and called an Intruder jet napalm strike to coordinates just north of the village. "Let them eat that!" cried Indian, walking through the carnage of Charlie Company. "Let them eat that!" he repeated.

Back on Hill 52, Doc heard the automatic arms fire and assumed the end would be near. He got himself ready for his move. All he had to do was lift his right shoulder blade and the grenade was armed. Five seconds later, "Sayonara, motherfucker!" He needed all of his reserve just to maintain consciousness.

The scuttle was coming closer and footsteps were approaching from over the hill. Indian and O'Malley had nearly given up when they saw the two bodies on Hill 52. O'Malley was a career soldier, but the sight of his brother was more than any man could take. He collapsed to his knees and grabbed his brother's lifeless body. "Joey, what have the motherfuckers done to you? Joey, I told Mom and Debbie I would take care of you. I wish it was me—I wish it was me!"

Indian recognized Doc immediately, but Doc was semi-delirious. He focused on the incoming soldier and readied himself for explosion when he recognized the uniform markings.

Then Indian's rugged features came into focus and panic ensued. Doc was booby-trapped. If he lost consciousness, Indian would inevitably pick him up and blow up. He had to hold it together and warn him. Doc's mouth moved but no words came out. His left lung was completely collapsed, and blood gushed out of his mouth with every attempted word.

He waved his hand wildly at Indian, who interpreted the sign as a cry for help. Doc realized that he had one shot to save both of their lives. He pointed to his mouth and waved Indian closer. With a final breath, clearing a large bolus of blood and froth from his pharynx, he whispered, "Grenade, grenade," while pointing to his right shoulder.

"I gotcha, buddy," answered Indian. "I may have gone to West Point, but I'm not stupid."

The ensuing sequence was a haze to Doc, but it was standard operating procedure for the Rangers.

"I've got a live munitions under a soldier!" shouted Indian. "I need a ninety-degree, thirty-yard perimeter due northeast of Hill 52. O'Malley, Joey is gone, buddy. I need you to take care of the other boys and I want you out of here. This grenade pin has been out for more than 15 minutes. You know what the boys in munitions say. 'If the pin is out, you might as well be walking with your dick out,' cause you're gonna get fucked—you don't know how much time you have."

O'Malley left with tears in his eyes. Joey was his only brother. Indian was also like a brother and the best 1st Louie he had. A Point guy with a heart of steel. Not many would evacuate their company to stay behind and clear a near-detonated grenade to save a soldier who was probably going to die. O'Malley, however, knew his job—he was a career grunt.

Indian's lacrosse experience paid off. After getting the all-clear from O'Malley, he slowly reached behind Doc's shoulder. Doc was the human equivalent of a 200-pound sack of potatoes by now. Indian felt the metal grenade handles. Doc started to rustle.

"Not now, buddy, just lay there and I'll do the work. You move and we both blow to shit!"

Doc seemed to understand. With the next fluid move, Indian pulled the grenade out and straight-arm whipped it about 20 yards into the air, throwing his body on top of Doc to protect him from any shrapnel. The only thing that saved their lives was Hill 52—the grenade went off one second after release.

Indian was hit by two pieces of shrapnel between his shoulder blades, one lying dangerously close to his spinal canal. He blew it off as a skin wound and carried Doc to the backup medic litter. It only hurt when he turned left! Hell, the medic litters were to the right of the hill and it was only seventy yards. His fatigues, however, were drenched in blood. He collapsed at the bottom of the hill. They were both carried out in litters. The Huey choppers arrived at 0735 hours.

Welcome to two hours in Vietnam. In the States, most people were having their scrambled eggs, listening to the news, drinking coffee.

Paul Kovalik woke up two days later in the Central Armed Forces Hospital, Saigon. His whole body hurt, but his first words were "Indian, where is Indian—he saved my life—I want to talk to Indian."

"Relax, Lieutenant Kovalik. You lost a lot of blood. You'll be fine—Dr. Pierce and Dr. Sample spent almost a whole night saving half your left kidney and most of your colon," said an attractive nurse, gently touching his shoulder. "You don't know how lucky you were. The bullet went through your retro peritoneum and we avoided a colostomy. Your chest tube is coming out tomorrow. The bullet went through your lung with minor pulmonary damage."

The nurse was a blonde. Her smile was magnificent, but most of the soldiers never got above her low-cut uniform neckline.

Normally, her presence would here immediately kindled a hormonal surge that would take horse tranquilizers to suppress. Now all Doc could think of was pain, his dead troops, and the man who threw his own body across his chest to save his life.

Senator Sumner played his son's heroics up for everything they were worth. This is a politician's dream come true—and it was an election year. David, on the other hand, wanted nothing to do with any medals or ceremony, but stateside, Paul Kovalik was front and center when David received the Congressional Medal of Honor, Silver Star, and Purple Heart. As a matter of fact, David Sumner denied any heroics even during the medal ceremony. He thought Doc deserved the Silver Star for protecting his troops in a mission against all odds. For the remainder of their lifelong close friendship, David Sumner would never admit to heroics or even mention the incident, even in private. It was just the way he was.

4

THE DISCOVERY

JAKE COULDN'T BELIEVE what he was seeing. Mrs. DeMarco's tumor-ridden liver was normal on all of the MRI images. He studied them over and over, making sure that all of the bases were covered, such as correct name, accession number, and date of birth. There was no doubt.

He immediately ran up to 6 West. The duty resident was a Lieutenant Jan Solomon, MD, a general internal medicine resident hoping to get into a radiology program. Jake was friendly with her. They had had several discussions over coffee about good radiology training programs.

"Hi, Jake," said Jan. "Guess things went bad at Tesla-6!"

"Yeah," responded Jake. "I just want to make sure Mrs. DeMarco's OK. I don't know what exactly happened down there, but we need a complete workup. Could you get an SMA 12 with a liver profile, cardiac echo, and EEG brainwave test?"

"Sure, Jake. The only thing is, Mrs. DeMarco looks a hell of a lot better now than before. Her jaundice is gone, her hypertension is stable, and when I listened to her heart, her leaky mitral valve was inaudible. I could hear it across the room before."

"Do me a favor, Jan, just run the tests STAT and get me the results ASAP. I've got a lot of things to present to Kovalik and I have to get my ducks in a row. I can't tell you what happened, because I don't really know," answered Jake.

The next twenty-four hours were hell. The pathology report on Sergeant DeMarco came in as "multi system organ failure with diffuse metastatic disease, adenocarcinoma of unknown primary." Jake gathered all of the data and came to the only scientific conclusion he could. To quote his Sherlock Holmes, "When you have excluded the impossible, whatever remains, however improbable, must be the truth." Maybe the dawn of a new era in scientific research, or then again, maybe another medical fuck-up of gargantuan proportions. Jake wondered if the great Dr. Ossler ever felt that way.

"Jake, I gave you a shot on the T-6 project. What the hell happened in there?" asked Kovalik in his administrative voice.

Jake threw down a 300-page chart and an X-ray folder containing five CAT scans and two MRIs on Kovalik's desk.

"Doctor Kovalik, I know that what happened to Sergeant DeMarco is a great tragedy, both personal as well as professional, but I have some concrete data here that is incredible. My theories on detection and tumor reversal with my new STIR pulse sequences at 6 Tesla were substantiated. Mrs. DeMarco showed not only tumor growth involution, but a complete remission. Look at the MRI. Tumor in the liver is gone. Not only that, but an echocardiogram shows that her leaking heart mitral valve is now normal and her Chem 12 profile shows that she has the lab values and metabolism of a 40-year-old!"

"And the sergeant's death, how do you account for that," asked Kovalik with a soft, sentimental voice.

"We'll look into that, General," responded Jake, knowing that he was on thin ice.

"You'll look into that! A healthy man goes into our T-6 experimental magnet. You break our documented regulation that no individuals other than the patient are allowed within the high magnetic field during scanning, and the man dies during a 20-minute pulse sequence which ends up lasting over two hours because you fell asleep at the console. I'm the one looking into that! You're suspended pending investigation, Captain Eriksson!"

"You can't do that, General. Look at the data—please! This isn't the first time a combination of science and accident has led to a major discovery. This may be the discovery of the century—more important than penicillin!"

Kovalik had the information Jake presented six hours before Jake even walked into his office. It was his job. Nothing went on in Walter Reed without Kovalik's knowledge, especially when it involved the T-6 project. He held an emergency meeting with Colonel Sam Smith earlier that morning.

"Sam, I have some preliminary data that is of the most sensitive nature. I want you to review this and get back to me in one hour," demanded Kovalik.

One hour later, Colonel Smith entered Kovalik's office with a look of awe on his face.

"Paul, I don't know exactly what happened in there, but there is no known medical explanation for Mrs. DeMarco and her recovery. She was dead, tumor all over. All data now point to not only a complete remission, but also a reversal of the aging process—we have to study this. It must be contained, Paul. We can't have a loose cannon like Eriksson running this show. It has to be a Pentagon operation, and I am fully capable of taking charge."

"Agreed," said Kovalik. Nothing more needed to be said. Jake Eriksson's career was to take a turn. As in Vietnam, Kovalik never liked sending men to their destiny. He was military, however. Sometimes unpleasant things needed to be done.

By the time Jake reached Kovalik's office, the script had been written. Kovalik's hand slipped to a button underneath his large oak desk. Two MPs immediately entered.

"Under Article 32 of the Uniform Code of Military Justice, I hereby relieve you of all duty pending a military investigation of your dereliction of duty and gross negligence resulting in the death of Master Sergeant Thomas DeMarco, USMC, retired," recited Kovalik. It was clear that he had done this before. It was also clear that he knew more than he let on!

Twenty-four hours later, in emergency session at the Pentagon, Kovalik presented the preliminary data. It was a rare mixed session made up of the Joint Chiefs, NSA, the FBI's top-secret Forensic and Medical Response Division, members of the Security Council of the Senate Judiciary Committee, as well as the top secret International Medical Division of the CDC. The meeting had no records, no minutes, and, in fact, never occurred.

"Kovalik, I'm an old military dog. You're going to have to explain this to me a little clearer and in plain English," said General Linder of the Joint Chiefs. "You've got some high-power officials in this room. We never even piss in the same bathroom, so could you please explain why this little experiment of yours is a matter of national security? It seems that you have nothing concrete."

"Gentlemen," started Kovalik deliberately. "What we are dealing with here is the potential transplantation of the vital life forces from one individual to another. In Eriksson's first experiment, he inadvertently drained something—I don't know what else to call it but the 'life force'—from a vibrant man into a cancer-ridden woman. He cured her of her disease and took at least ten years off her life. She is metabolically ten years younger. The implications of this Dorian Gray scenario are immense. The sacrifice of the donor is ultimate. The donor dies! We may have the cure for all disease at hand, but at what moral and ethical cost, gentlemen?"

"What if we put a Navy Seal into the chamber and transfer this 'vital force' into him?" asked General Pachinko of the UDT/Seal division. "Do we get a super-being—an invincible soldier with an enhanced immune system and powers of self-healing that we can't even comprehend? These are the moral and ethical questions we have to understand and face before the public and scientific community take hold of this and do what they do best, fuck it up!"

The group was riveted by the information they were hearing. This was the incarnation of Hitler's experiments, but with concrete results. Kovalik continued—

"This is a military project which has the potential of becoming a national security risk. I ask that we classify this project and that my elite team be allowed to continue the research with no questions and at all cost."

Kovalik was excused and the chamber went into executive session for 45 minutes. He was then asked to step in, and Senator Mitchum from the Senate Judiciary Commission spoke for all concerned.

"This project is hereby classified Top Secret and named 'Lazarus.' General Kovalik, you are in command. Security measures are Extreme. This committee will get weekly reports in PGP maximum encryption through our double firewall Web server. I will leave procurement of 'volunteers' and Eriksson's future at your disposal. You will have full NSA, FBI, CIA, Secret Service, and Military Special Services cooperation at your disposal—on a need-to-know basis, of course. I assume there are no further questions?"

Within 15 minutes of Eriksson's arrest, his passes were erased, all data in his office confiscated, and all sites in the hospital he frequented inspected with a fine-tooth comb for data, diskettes, or anything dealing with Project Lazarus. Eriksson's article 32 was a well-orchestrated play. His only hope was military law—the Judge Advocate's office, the JAG. He knew that the military code, especially an Article 32, assumed innocence until it was strongly proven otherwise.

He would have the benefit of the doubt—he thought! Then he saw the JAG assigned to him. The kid looked like he had just started shaving yesterday. He was the poorest example of a lawyer the military could muster. Bottom of his class at Southern Mississippi Tech prior to entering the military court system.

"Look, Captain Eriksson, your case is hopeless," said the young JAG lawyer. "They've got you on Article 92, failure to obey an order or regulation, for allowing Sergeant DeMarco in the magnet room; Article 93, cruelty and maltreatment towards Sergeant and Mrs. DeMarco; Article 115, for malingering and falling asleep on duty; Article 124, maiming; Article 128, assault—"

"Wait a fucking minute!" cried Jake. "Those Articles are a bunch of military misdemeanors. You could probably plead me down to negligence for falling asleep on duty. You just told me I have to either take a dishonorable discharge, which means I automatically get this charged to my record as a felony, and lose my medical license—or hope for a military court martial with some leniency. That means I can no longer practice medicine in the military. I'll get transferred to some shithole as a private to serve out my 12-year enlistment. None of this makes sense!"

"You didn't let me finish, Captain," said the JAG lawyer impatiently. "I'm the best you've got, buddy, and the charges I haven't mentioned yet include an Article 112, drunk on duty; Article 111, operating military equipment while drunk; and Article 118, negligent murder for allowing Sergeant DeMarco into the MRI unit when you knew he had a pacemaker—directly resulting in his death."

"Are you crazy?" shouted Jake. "I wasn't drunk! They never took an alcohol blood test on me! Where did this pacemaker shit come from? I asked Sergeant DeMarco personally if he had any cardiac problems or a pacemaker—it's routine. The man was as healthy as a mule!"

The lawyer dropped three large binders full of data on the table and quietly whispered, "Look, Jake, I'm on your side, but the data is in front of you. Here is a deposition from a Lieutenant Susan Carlson saying that you and she were drinking heavily prior to your going on duty on the T-6 magnet. Here's a lab report showing your blood alcohol level well above the intoxication zone, and here's the autopsy report on Sergeant DeMarco—'CAUSE OF DEATH: MAGNETIC FIELD INDUCED PACEMAKER MALFUNCTION WITH RESULTING ASYSTOLE AND MYOCARDIAL INFARCTION.' Give it up, Jake," he pleaded. "I'll try to get you down to involuntary manslaughter; you'll be court-martialed, transferred, and you'll get your life back in 12 years. The other option is life in prison—you have no choice, Jake, you have no choice."

Jake's eyes welled up. He has never in his life experienced such a feeling of lack of control. He was the best at everything. Things like this never happened to the great Jake Eriksson.

He had discovered the Fountain of Youth, but forgotten to take the first drink! Pounding both fists on the table with a resonating boom that startled the JAG counselor, Jake shouted just one word—"Kovalik!"

5

THE WASHINGTON DC VA HOSPITAL

IF WALTER REED Army Medical Center is considered the army's most prestigious medical facility, the Washington Veterans Administration has the honor of being the last place you would ever want to go for health care. Not that the VA system was all that bad—but the Washington "Venereal" Administration was!

When Jake's lawyer plea-bargained a demotion and VA assignment, rather than prison prior to formal court martial, Jake thought he would go to the ritzy Baltimore VA. As he walked up the decrepit wooden stairs, he realized that he was just stationed in purgatory—and Hell was just around the corner!

"So you're Captain—excuse me, Private—Jake Eriksson, MD," smirked Captain Jackson, Commanding Officer of the VA. "We don't often get Ivy League types around here, but then again, it's hard to get good help in the military these days. I'm gonna make sure that when you leave here, your skills at making beds, sweeping floors, and cleaning bedpans is up to my military standards. Got that, Private?"

Jake swallowed hard. Jackson was the kind of doctor who could only make it in the VA system. As a matter of fact, he was CO of the lowliest VA in the country. Jake was well aware of his tenuous position and answered the only way he could. "Yes, sir, Captain Jackson."

"That's mighty white of you. You see, while you are in this VA you're in the good graces of God and me. God may forgive you, but if I as much as whisper, you're going to military prison. If I catch you practicing medicine, you're going to military prison. Do you know what they do to little Ivy League white boys like you in the Texas Pen?"

The question was rhetorical. Jake's mandatory "No, sir" was a matter of military necessity, but it prompted a fifteen-minute description of the pivotal scenes from *Deliverance*.

Jake immediately understood the rules. He was dealing with the military version of affirmative action, often called "affirmative inaction." Doctors like Jackson had no shot in the private sector. In the military there was always a spot. He was a throwback to an era that never was, and he was reliving it by torturing Jake, an Ivy League preppie. Jake did the best he could.

All in all, Jake's time in the VA wasn't that bad. He became friendly with most of the other orderlies, and the other VA docs were often grateful when Jake interpreted their X-rays and helped them with complex diagnoses. It was somewhat humorous to Jake; the only problem was, he was laughing at his own life.

Most of the VA patients were guys with smoke-related lung disease, cancer, old syphilis, and old Korean and World War II vets who had nowhere else to go in life. For the most part, they were your typical army grunts. Salt-of-the-earth working guys, down on their luck.

Interesting that everyone in that VA was plain old down on luck—from the CO all the way to the poor bastards in the terminal ward. Every other word was "fuck" and "gimme a cigarette." Frank Wright was the exception. Frank had been a staff sergeant in the Korean War. He had a great sense of humor and often spoke to Jake in an honest and straightforward manner. He was a self-taught man, exceptionally bright and insightful. He had one big problem—terminal metastatic lung cancer. Jake helped him with his medical problems, off the record, of course, and Frank helped Jake with life. Jake often confided in Frank in a way he never could with his own father.

He told Frank his story, down to the last detail. Frank's attention never wavered. Although the terms were somewhat alien to Frank, he understood everything. He knew the military like the back of his hand. He predicted the ending even before Jake could spit it out of his mouth. A classic military "black" operation!

"Listen, Jake," said Frank in his usual sage tone. "If you give up now, you let them fuck you. You're no better than they are. You discovered something wonderful. Fight for your life. I can tell you're a good guy at heart. Look at me—I'm riddled with the cancer, but I'm going down fighting. If your invention is real, guys like me have the potential of being cured. You owe it to yourself—you owe it to me!"

"I know, Frank, but they have me pinned. I don't even know where to start. I've been thinking of this for over a month now. What I need to do is prove to the brass that this is some sort of cover-up. I've got to get back into my lab to get my records and the evidence." Jake stared down at the rotting wooden floor planks of the solarium.

"Are you kidding, Jake? Who the hell do you think is behind this? This baby smells like military cover-up all the way. Only the Pentagon and NSC can pull this type of smoke-screen and nail you to the wall. Believe me, I've done some stuff for the military I'm not too proud of. I put in five years in SpecOps. This is a spook operation all the way. I still got some friends in the Pentagon and my daughter works for the NSC—computer encryption division. I'm gonna check things out. Jake, she's something, my daughter. I want you to meet her this Saturday."

"What are you talking about, Frank?" asked Jake with a look of concern on his face. Frank occasionally rambled. Jake attributed it to metastasis to the frontal cortex. Patients get a little goofy with frontal mets.

It was a magnificent fall weekend. Even the VA grounds looked serene and peaceful. Saturdays were special—visiting day. Valerie Wright always entered the ivy-covered gates with trepidation. Dad looked worse with each visit. A vibrant, strong military man reduced to a skeletonized shadow of his former self. She was his baby and she had always adored him.

It was as though his demeanor melted in her presence. Val had a hypnotic effect on him, and she knew that every moment she spent with Dad was precious.

After Mom died two years ago, Valerie knew that her father lost most of himself. He had smoked two packs a day for 35 years. The cancer did not surprise her. Nonetheless, seeing him was always heartbreaking. She knew they had little time.

"Val, baby doll!" shouted Frank as she entered the South Wing Sanatorium. The sunbeams brilliantly glimmered into the usual moribund room, but they could not hold a candle to the smile on Frank's face when he gazed upon his daughter.

"You look good, Dad," responded Val. Actually, he looked terrible.

"I missed your visits. Haven't seen you for a month."

"Dad, I visited you two weeks ago and told you I was going to Nevada for two weeks on a government computer job," said Val quietly while gently patting her father's hand. His memory was going. It was the cancer. Valerie looked away for a second and discreetly wiped a small tear from the corner of her right eye. "That's okay, Pop, I'm here now and that's all that matters. I won't miss visiting day again."

"Never mind. We have a project! I want you to meet somebody. Somebody in trouble. A doc here who has been nice to me but got a Pentagon screw job, Val. Trust me, baby, this is a good guy. He discovered something that can possibly help me, but we gotta help him get out of this mess." Frank was getting agitated.

Valerie knew the cancer had spread to his brain. This was the start of the downward spiral. He wasn't making sense. He was rambling. This was the hardest part of her recent visits. Dad would be OK initially and then enter some sort of delusional state that deeply distressed her.

"This isn't the cancer speaking, Val," shouted Frank. You have to believe me and help us out. I've got some calls in to Pentagon brass who owe me big. You have computer access that can break this wide open."

Jake had entered the far end of the room, starting his cleanup rounds. Frank was looking straight ahead and Valerie's back was towards Jake.

"Jake!" shouted Frank, "Come here, I want you to meet someone very special!" Valerie turned to look at this orderly with a miracle cure.

As Jake looked over Valerie's face, he knew immediately that this was not his year. As Bogie said in *Casablanca*, of all the gin joints in all the towns in all the world, she walks into mine." His jaw dropped as he realized that Frank's Valerie was Val. Not just any Val but his Val. About the only girl in his life he regretted treating like shit. The only girl in his life who scared him because she was capable of capturing his heart and almost had.

Harvard was tough, and Jake was a pre-med major with a minor in physics. Val was in his lab course. She was an MIT undergrad taking her prerequisites in Visual Basic/C+, an upper-level programming course. Harvard and MIT shared some curriculum courses.

The moment he saw her, he knew he had met his match. She was brilliant. Jet-black hair, incredible lips, and a smile that always looked like she was in control. It was as if Val always knew the answer—and Jake rarely knew the question!

It was like an open flame meeting gasoline. Combustion was inevitable—the question was, who was going to get burned?

Valerie's friends warned her of Jake's reputation, but it was like a nature documentary—like the call of animal magnetism couldn't be stopped. Someone was going to get screwed, and that someone ended up being Val, literally and figuratively.

The problem wasn't that Jake didn't love her. The problem was that he did, but nothing was going to get in the way of medical school, not even the girl of his dreams. Jake could have dealt with the situation in many different mature ways. He could have even used the "we can still be friends" line. His actual words, however, were "I only screwed you so that you would continue helping me get through Visual Basic."

He felt that it was more honorable to just break things clean, the way Clark Gable did it in *Gone with the Wind* and Rick did it at the airport in *Casablanca*. He often lived his life by quoting movie monologues.

The results were the same, but after a one-year relationship, Val never got over her bitterness and Jake never got over his regret. He often thought of calling her and explaining, but he never figured out just what the explanation was—other than "I was an asshole, I was young, and I loved you at the wrong time in my life and I couldn't deal with commitment." The call never happened, and now payback time was here! Jake had to find out the hard way that doing the right thing often only hurt once, but doing the wrong thing kept on hurting.

Valerie's reaction was somewhat more visceral. Her right palm reached out and slapped Jake across his face so hard that a small drop of blood dripped down the corner of his mouth.

"Jake the snake! You son of a bitch! I've been waiting to do that for seven long years!" shouted Valerie. "I've been following your career. Every time I open the *Harvard Gazette*, your damn picture reminds me what a shit you were. Graduated Phi Beta Kappa from undergrad, AOA from medical school with a combined MD/PhD in electro-physiology. The first resident to finish a combined Radiology and Neurology residency at Mass General Hospital."

"I was waiting for the apology call for six months. I felt like a minor league pitcher waiting to play in 'the big show.' Nobody ever hurt me the way you did. Then it dawned on me that you were just a self-serving bastard and I hate you Jake! I—hate—you!"

"Guess I should have called, even if I had nothing to say," thought Jake as he rubbed the left side of his face.

Frank was just observing this somewhat interesting interaction. He was old enough to recognize passion, and he knew his daughter better than anyone on earth. He saw the gleam in their eyes. Love and hate are similar emotions during courtship, and Val was a big girl, capable of protecting herself. Jake was a bit brash and young, sowing his oats. God knows Frank had been there before, until he met Val's mother, and oh, how alike mother and daughter were. Frank knew Jake had no chance, so he smiled and said the only thing he could—"I see you two have met!"

The next day, Jake was a little hesitant approaching Frank. Valerie must have divulged her part of the relationship, and Jake really had no shot regardless of what side was heard. Most men have a love-'em-and-leave-'em story. Most men have hurt a poor unsuspecting girl, perhaps with the best of initial intentions, but with the same results nonetheless. Jake just happened to make a habit of what he called the "science of uncommitment."

"You know, you can break up a relationship many ways," Jake would say. "You can split up and pretend to be best of friends, you can play the sensitive sap and admit to making a terrible mistake, you can use the old 'fallen out of love' line, but I always went for the most honorable of breakups—I never called the bitch again!"

This worked well on the whole, especially when talking machismo with other guys—but then there was Val! Jake had never fallen in love with any woman before. His father was a poor example of fidelity, and as the old adage says, "The apple doesn't fall far from the tree"—but then there was Val!

Jake had never met a woman who could equal his ego, his aggression, his intellect—who could dominate the situation yet be feminine and sensuous. Who could both dominate and be dominated at the same time. Val was all of those things and more.

Val's outlook was actually very similar. She had never met a man as arrogant and self-reliant as Jake. Normally, those attributes would disgust her, but Jake was different and her guard was down. Jake made her laugh. If only more men understood the power of laughter.

As with most relationships, the candle that burns hot burns briefly, and it was just a matter of time. They were young and one of them was bound to get scared, and Jake was the one.

Of all the women Jake dumped, Val was still a lucid memory. She was the one he wished he had met later in life. She never left his memory, and the sting of her slap was doubly felt. His relationship with Frank was very important to him. It was the only thing maintaining his humanity and dignity during this trial by dehumanization. Here was an intelligent man willing to listen, willing to look beyond his orderly duties and believe him. Perhaps it was the cancer, but Jake could see through Frank's disease. He could tell when Frank was lucid

Frank was like the father he never had. He listened to Jake's problems and offered the wisdom of his years. Not "silver spoon" years but hard years, loving years with a marriage that ended in tragedy. Time spent with hard work putting their only daughter through MIT, a wife suffering from breast cancer with two tragic years of chemotherapy.

It then occurred to Jake while doing some simple arith-
metic. His relationship and eventual breakup with Val occurred during her mother's illness. That didn't help—what a
shit he was! Frank had every right to deck him. But this time
he would not cop out. He would face Frank like a man.

It was a chilly fall day and Jake felt an even greater chill
that next day, knowing that he had sanatorium duty and
that Frank would be there. They made eye contact almost
immediately. Frank was sitting in his favorite window seat.

"Jake, would you get me a hot cup of java?" said Frank
with a sheepish smile.

Jake returned within moments with a tall styrofoam cup,
just the way Frank liked it—black with four spoons of sugar.

"Jake, you son of a bitch. Not enough sugar!" scowled
Frank.

"What's the matter, Pops, the spoon won't stand in the
black gut rot?" asked Jake with a smile. It was their usual
exchange. Jake got the message. Frank was not going to make
what he saw with Val into a problem.

"Sit down, son," commanded Frank with a tone he had
used on enlisted men hundreds of times before. Jake sat with
no comment. It reminded him of Kovalik, his commanding
officer at Walter Reed. It was the tone of someone who has
seen combat and conquered himself as well as the enemy.

"Jake, you're a talented man. You're also brash, unfocused,
disrespectful, a womanizer, and most of all a waste of a
brilliant career. You can save the lives of grunts like me, but
you're too busy chasing tail to realize your own potential. Jake,
stop trying to please your father. Stop running away—you're
better than that.

"Val told me of what happened—at least the parts she
could tell her old fart father. It was easy to make up the parts
she didn't tell me. You and I told each other a lot of good
stories in the past few months—I just wish one of them hadn't

been about my daughter! But she's a big girl and I'm sure she has some good stories of her own. Anyway, Jake, I never had a son. If I had one, I would like him to be like you.

"The fight you and Val had is not important. I did a lot of things I shouldn't have. I just want to tell you that I gave you a good word back there after she tried to dislocate your jaw—she's got her mother's right hook, that one does! And her mother's eyes and will. Guys like you and I don't have a shot with women like that. I can see her mother in her eyes. I can see my heart in you. Don't give up, Jake! Not with anything. Don't let the assholes get away with the cover-up. Don't let my daughter get away—I know she loves you still—I can feel it!"

Jake responded with a simple "Yes, Frank, I understand."

Frank had "the look." In medical school, everyone learned of "the look." Few people outside of medicine can identify that intangible appearance a human being has when about to die. It's a look of passing, a sad look of equilibrium with the mortal world. Jake knew and understood. He now understood the pain he never allowed himself to feel for any patient—any friend—any woman! This old tattooed man taught him what nobody else could.

Frank died peacefully that night, Val by his side. Jake walked by the room several times, but was afraid to look Val in the eyes—not yet. He wanted to say goodbye to Frank, but there was no opportunity.

6

ARLINGTON NATIONAL CEMETERY

DECEMBER 18 WAS a cold, rainy Washington day. Master Sergeant Frank William Wright III was laid to rest with a hero's 21-gun salute. He was a decorated Korean War veteran who had received both a Silver Star and Purple Heart in combat.

Jake had to attend the funeral but did so from the back. He did not want to be noticed and he certainly did not want another scene with Val. He doubted that Frank's vision of both of them together again was reality—not after that slap in the face. Women tend not to forget things like being dumped. Jake did, however, underestimate the power of love. As the French say, "Vive la guerre" and "Vive l'amour." They often said them in the same sentence. Then again, the French think they invented everything related to love!

Jake scanned the attendants. His obvious focus was Val, dressed in black with a black veil partially covering teary eyes and an umbrella held by someone Jake recognized as Director of the NSC. The Vice President of the United States was in the first row, as was the Secretary of State. Paul Kovalik was in the gallery immediately across from the bereaved. He had never met Val, but certainly wanted to pay his respects to a decorated national hero. Kovalik had served his country with pride. To him, the death of a decorated war hero was always somber and worthy of his fullest respect. Interesting how fate brings people together.

Val looked sad but more beautiful than ever. The radiance of her tear-filled eyes, the natural cherubic blush of her lips. Jake had repressed these feelings before—but then he was on top of the world. Now he was nothing. He'd lost his medical degree, any hope of research, and the rights to what could have been be one of the most important discoveries of the century—and Paul Kovalik, his nemesis, was standing in front of him. Frank was right. He couldn't give up! He had nothing to lose anymore.

After the brief ceremony, Jake started walking towards the gate. The last few months had been rough on the old bank account. He'd had to sell his car just to make the payments on his apartment next to the VA. A private's salary is not one that can support a BMW 328i. He smiled at the thought. "If Dad could see me now. All of his predictions right on the money. The great fucking Karnack, that's what he is—the great fucking Karnack."

By the time he approached the gate, the early winter drizzle had become a good old Washington downpour, but Jake really didn't care. The walk would help him clear his mind.

The black limousine pulled up to him about a hundred feet from the gate. As the window rolled down, Jake gazed at Val's sullen eyes. "Get in, asshole! I don't feel like going to two funerals."

Jake kept walking, past the gate and into the street. The train station was about four blocks from the entrance. Val's limo paced him for two blocks until Jake suddenly stopped and looked at the passenger window. "You know, I don't need your pity, Val," he said. "I respected your father. He listened, and for the brief time I knew him, he was more of a father to me than my own father, so I don't need your pity or any more anger."

"Get in the car, Jake," whispered Valerie. "Neither of us has much more to give today. You used to like bourbon—Jack and Coke, if I remember right. I always thought that was funny. I don't think I have Coke in my apartment, but I think I still have the bottle of Jack Daniel's you opened seven years ago."

Valerie's gentle expression was a surprise to Jake. He opened the door and got into the back seat. He was soaked.

"You held onto the bottle?" asked Jake with a subtle innocent smirk.

"Yeah, well, I had to have something personal to hit you with the next time I saw you. Besides, I swore I would never date anyone who drank bourbon again!"

Val was never one for neatness. The living room of her Georgetown brownstone was cluttered with hundreds of papers, a wall unit full of computers including an Ultra Spark workstation, an NT workstation, and a Mac G4 workstation. The couch had a comfy pillow with a ThinkPad laptop, opened between the seams of the two seat cushions.

There were dishes in the sink and Chinese food cartons on the kitchen table, and a peek into the bedroom revealed an unmade bed with the comforter sprawled on the bedpost.

Jake smiled as he entered the apartment. He was just glad to get out of the wet and cold. He did remember how incompatible they were while dating. He kept on cleaning her dorm room and she never understood why he would disrupt her perfectly logical filing system. "You sure you have enough computers, Val?" he asked.

"When you work for the NSC and head Security Systems and Encryption, you get the toys of the trade—you know about toys of the trade, don't you Jake? Was that what I was?"

"Ouch," said Jake, "I thought we were going to keep this civil."

"Sorry, it's just been a long day. You've been good to dad and you didn't deserve that. He asked me to thank you for your kindness. He loved your stories and told them to me.

Most of them were probably his brain mets speaking—stuff about life force transfer and government plots, but they did keep him busy while I was on assignment in Nevada.

"What ever happened, Jake? What ever happened to that arrogant unstoppable pre-med that never stumbled or fell? You were a shooting star. How did you end up a orderly in the VA?"

Jake just looked at her with a smile. He didn't believe it himself. "My story is screwed up, but your father was telling the truth. They weren't delusional, Val. They were the truth. The truth."

Val's expression suddenly changed. Jake could see he had hit a nerve. They certainly had much history to reconcile, and even a dormant volcano can erupt—and Val was anything but dormant.

"You ran out of truth a long time ago, Jake," said Val with a quiet quiver in her voice. "You use people, Jake. A part of me still cares, but a part of me can never forget what a shit you were. Are you still using those awful lines about your mother to pick up women, or was that a college thing?"

Val couldn't actually remember forming the words. They just came out of her mouth. She had no reserve left. Somehow, "truth" and "Jake" in the same sentence triggered her. During their romance, there had been a lot of "truths." Now she had lost her last parent and the object of her affliction was in front of her talking about the "truth."

"Jake, you son of a bitch, you couldn't recognize the truth if it hit you on the head. Don't start lying about my father now. Let me have my dignity at least for this moment," Val said, sobbing.

Jake just got up and got his coat. He was still using those lines, and he never gave it much thought. Val knew him better than he had thought. He just wanted to go over and comfort her, but it was time to leave. Even Jake the Snake could not make this right. There were no more lines, and for once in his life he wished he could tell the truth and actually be believed.

"I'm sorry, Val." Those were the only words he could whisper as he walked out the door.

The slow walk down the brownstone steps was strange for Jake. For once in his life, he realized that he had nothing. No family to speak of, no friends, no real job, and no career. Just a pending court martial, or better yet, military prison for something he hadn't done.

It then dawned on him that he had missed the last train back to his apartment and didn't even have enough money for a cab. With a bitter smile, he sat on the cold, wet bottom step and started thinking about Frank.

"You were wrong about me, Frank," said Jake to himself. "I am a loser."

In the brief time they knew each other, Frank had shown him a level of kindness and understanding Jake never had from his own father. What a twist of fate—Frank was Val's father! Even Shakespeare couldn't have thought this one up. The play could have been named *Taming of the Screwed*.

The smile only lasted a millisecond. Jake placed his head in his hands and tears started welling in his eyes. "Frank, you old son of a bitch, I'm going to miss you. I'm going to miss you. I know I need strength now, but I just don't know where to reach."

The last time he remembered crying was in elementary school when he dropped the game-winning pass in the end zone. He wanted to make Dad so proud, but the wet ball slipped out of his hands. On the ride home, his father slapped him across the face.

"Jake," he said. "That's not for dropping the ball. That's for crying!" Jake never cried again—until now! He just sat on the brick stairs, overcoat collar up, leaning on the banister. He had nowhere to go.

Perhaps it had been minutes, perhaps hours. Jake had no idea. He just heard the door behind him open and a female voice. "You have two choices: you can come back in or I can call the police on you as a vagrant."

Val's voice was somewhere between anger and frustration. Even she didn't know what to feel. "You don't even have enough money for a cab, do you?" she asked.

Answering was pointless. Jake just walked in. He had actually spent over two hours in the cold. His lips were blue and he was shaking uncontrollably. Val had some of her Dad's clothes in the closet.

It's hard taking that final step and giving away the last physical remnant of your father. Jake looked a little silly in tight pajamas and a robe, but two blankets and a cup of Earl Grey tea finally got his shakes under control.

"Jake, just lie down on the couch and keep my laptop company," said Val. "Let's just call a truce and I'll drive you to the VA in the morning."

Jake drank the cup of tea within minutes. He looked pathetic, but Val saw a vulnerable side that she had never known existed. Perhaps Jake had learned something.

"Thanks, Val. You know it's hard for me to be here. It's hard to look at yourself in the mirror sometimes—"

"Never mind," she said. "I put some of your famous bourbon in that tea. The last thing I need is 'The True Confessions of Jake the Snake while Driving under the Influence.' " She smiled and tucked him in on the couch.

Val stared at Jake's sleeping face in the shadow of the flickering fireplace light. She was sipping on tea and thinking of her losses. Jake was certainly among them. She had never really understood the turn of events seven years ago. That's what hurt so much. Val was a strong woman. She had never let men get to her before, and she certainly wouldn't again. But she was younger then. And so was Jake!

She was the best intuitive mathematician the MIT computer science department ever had. She hung out with the hackers but never really entered the world of dark hacking—she found it too easy. At 23, she broke into the State Department computer. They still don't know. Hacking is the art of entry without detection. It is the art of extreme cover. Every move is cleaned before exit.

Whereas many hackers have malicious intent, Val entered just for the fun of it. She had the ability to enter from any computer. Professor Alexander Romanoff was her mentor and counselor. She was his proudest accomplishment, but he often felt he had to rein her in. He and Val got into an especially strong argument one afternoon about the role of government in the code of computer ethics. Romanoff should have known better!

Professor Romanoff heard the knock on his door in the Boston North Shore suburb of Swampscott at 7 am. Two men, dressed in black.

"Professor Romanoff, we are sorry to intrude," the taller man said with a monotone only taught by the Feds. "Agent Dougherty, State Department. Would you please come with us?"

The request was not a request. The State Department badge clearly identified the agent. Romanoff spent the next sixteen hours getting grilled in a dark room with only one light—pointing at him.

He was innocent, of course. It appeared that someone cracked the State Department computer using what hackers called the scenic route. Some hacker used 17 servers, starting in the Netherlands and finally exiting through Melbourne directly into the State Department computer via a cash machine. The ATM was down the hall from the most secure computer in the world. It seems that the crossover Cisco router handled the ATM T1 line as well as the security mainframe. The origin call was traced to Romanoff's office. Three people were fired in the State Department. Romanoff was cleared, but he knew only one person in MIT capable of breaking the ultimate hacker taboo—"You don't mess with the government." That was Val. The fact that they had had a minor disagreement the day before about a piece of code Val wrote for NASA was not coincidental.

"Val, you little bitch! Do you know what those assholes did to me?" shouted Romanoff. Val and the professor actually had a great relationship, but Val had crossed the line on this one!

"Whatever do you mean, Professor?" asked Val with a sheepish grin. "Mary told me you needed some time away and that you went to the Cape cottage for the weekend."

Mary was the professor's wife. She had been like a second mother to Val, especially after her mother died. Mary recognized the academic thrill her husband got from Val. It's rare to get a real prodigy in MIT, and there's nothing Mary loved more than a humbling experience for Herr Professor Romanoff. They laughed so hard the night of the interrogation that their sides almost burst.

"Now, Val," continued the Professor, trying to contain his anger. "The fact that you successfully broke into the State Department doesn't surprise me. The fact that you did it through an ATM machine doesn't surprise me. But Val, the fact that you got caught and they traced it back to me—that surprises me. That is, unless you wanted to get caught. That hurts, Val, that really hurts."

As fate would have it, Val became the lead programmer and network designer for the NSA. She was often on loan to other government agencies. She was the best, and in the world of hackers, Val always said, it takes one to know one.

Val couldn't sleep that night. At around midnight, she got herself to do something she was hesitant to do since her father's death. In his belongings lay a journal with a note carefully attached to the front. Dad's handwriting was unmistakable. "I love you, Val, open this," signed "Dad."

The rest of the night was a blur. She carefully read every entry in Dad's diary. Dad had a military engineering background and was a stickler for detail. The entries were carefully annotated and even included diagrams. The entries were clearly not the ravings of a cancer-riddled individual, but carefully written accounts of the most incredible story Val had ever read. The explanation was there!

The entries could have been entitled "The Rise and Fall of Jake Eriksson." Val understood but still needed some concrete evidence.

While Jake slept in a deep febrile trance, fed by the alcohol-laced tea, the computer screens in the small Georgetown apartment came to life with activity.

"Let's see if the old hacker still has what it takes," muttered Val with an evil smirk on her face. She started on the Unix workstation. Walter Reed was a government installation. She wrote the encryption code for all military applications. Dollars-to-doughnuts, Walter Reed was using her security algorithms.

The only problem was that her government encryption assignment was simple—make it tamper-proof. That meant to everyone, including government insiders.

It was! 512-bit wavelet encryption was not even written about in the highest-level hacker primers. It was her invention. By Val's own estimates, it would take the Pentagon 150 years of nonstop computer processing to decipher her code.

As with most hackers, however, the ultimate rule was called "all but you." Val had a nasty habit of putting a rear entry point in all of her programs, so complex that only one person could access it, and that was Val.

The spook business was one where very few prisoners were taken. Professor Romanoff continually reminded Val of that and was vehemently opposed to her wasting her talents on spy stuff. "Watch your pretty little ass, Val," were his departing words. Val never forgot.

The back door she planted into the government security program wasn't the problem. Getting through on a secure server was easy. Your average high school hacker could find at least two hundred European and Eastern Bloc servers that made tracing difficult, although not impossible. Her real problem was the hunter-killers she programmed into the security host computer. These were the digital equivalents of homing missiles. Within two minutes of any file being accessed, a hunter-killer was launched demanding a positive internal ID.

Val's only option was to switch terminals within that time to avoid detection. She then had to simultaneously launch her own digital cleanup robot, which she called "Dust Buster." This designer probe was a virus that completely erased all traces of tampering and then self-destructed on exit. Even the file directory structure was altered. In the wrong hands, it could wipe out an entire computer network in seconds. Romanoff would have been proud.

Unfortunately, Val could only identify the exact number of on-site terminals once logged on. This gave her little precious time for exploration. There were three computer terminals. The math was simple. Val had only six minutes to get into the Walter Reed medical database and then to search out any information on Jake Eriksson and the Tesla 6 project.

She was afraid of that. Plan B was the hacker's last resort when given severe time constraints. Known as a "Sherlock Holmes," it was actually quite elegant. Val programmed search parameters prior to security entry. These were definitions, which the Sherlock probe would search for. It included all erased files still on the drive. She got the file names out of her father's journal. The probe would then go in and down-load all files fitting the search definitions, change terminals at 1 minute 59 seconds, and then continue until time ran out. Dust Buster was one second behind, erasing all evidence of entry. It was something like Yahoo on steroids.

Val hated this type of hacking because she had no ability to maneuver. However, her first Sherlock definition was "ALL PASS CODES." She knew this would take very little time and could be used later in case she had to get inside again, up close and personal.

It took 25 minutes to travel around the world via multiple secure computer hosts. Her entry point was Amazon.com. Not only was that server gigantic and easy to hack, she further covered her tracks by piggyback, ordering one thousand copies of to the last thousand people who sent in orders from Iran. *Ronald Reagan: An American Hero.* A girl's gotta have some fun.

The download was 497 pages, mostly junk. Val was experienced enough to be able to sift through it rapidly. The information she needed started on page 442—

> ###ENTRY--T-6 MAINFRAME: CLASSIFIED/PROJECT LAZARUS
>
> ###SUBJECT:0001/JAKE ERIKSSON-ERASE SUBFOLDER/C:KOVALIK-ENTRYON DVDROM ARCHIVE/T-6-JUKEBOX-OFFLINE/PGP256 WAVELET
>
> ###SUBJECT:0002/J DEMARCO-ERASE SUBFOLDER/ C:KOVALIK-ENTRYON DVDROM ARCHIVE/ T-6-JUKEBOX-OFFLINE/PGP256 WAVELET/BLACKICE

On page 488, things started to get interesting—

> ###BACKUP ALL ENTRIES: ERIKSSON,JACOB/T-6 JUKEBOX-OFFLINE/PGP256 WAVELET/BLACKICE
>
> ###ERASE ALL ENTRIES/SEARCH PARAMETERS: ERIKSSON,JACOB/ALL DIRECTORIES/FULL

NETWORK SEARCH/PRIORITY CODE
###2343145XNYX###PKOVALIK

But on page 497, reality finally struck—

###MEDREC DATABASE/SECURITY OVERRIDE
%$$#%$%/PARAMETER CHANGE/ERIKSSON,J/
SS#1320067436/BLOOD ALCOHOL/X2.5

###MEDREC DATABASE/PARAMETER CHANGE/
DEMARCO,T/SS#001457573/ADD/LINE56/PRIOR
HISTORY OF VENTRICULAR BRADYCARDIA AND
ASYSTOLE WITH IMPLANTED PACEMAKER/LINE 286/
CHANGE CAUSE OF DEATH TO:MAGNETIC FIELD
INDUCED PACEMAKER MALFUNCTION WITH
INDUCED ASYSTOLE AND CARDIAC ARREST/END—

And Val remembered John 11:38–44. They led Jesus to
the tomb of Lazarus and Jesus said, "Remove the stone . . .
if you believe, you will see the glory of God." Jesus cried,
"Lazarus, come forth"—and Lazarus came forth in his burial
wrappings, awakened from the dead.

Morning came to Val only two hours later. Val never quite
made it to the bedroom but fell asleep on a lounger next to her
computers, 497 pages of printout still on her lap. Jake started
stirring on the couch and the noise awakened her.

"Man, I feel like shit," muttered Jake in a hoarse voice.
"Sorry about last night—guess my story is hard to believe."

"Actually, it's impossible to believe," responded Val. "I
have one problem. After reading Dad's journal entries, I was
stupid enough to hack into the Walter Reed medical database.
I got into the T-6 server."

"Val, nobody can get into the server. I remember the
security clearance it took to get me on the project. The only
thing missing was the rubber gloves in my rectum! They told
me the computer security measures were identical to the NSA
and Pentagon."

"Lucky I wrote the program," smiled Val. "My only problem was that it's hard to hack yourself—kind of like reading your own mind. Anyway Jake, you don't exist on the T-6 project. You were erased. The charges against you were drummed up as an accident which occurred on the conventional Walter Reed 1.5 Tesla magnet."

"That's bullshit, Val!"

"I know, Jake," answered Val in a softer voice. "There's more. Take a look at these printouts. If I get caught, it's about forty years in the federal penitentiary, but I had to do it for Dad. Does Project Lazarus mean anything to you?"

"Never heard of it," answered Jake.

"Well, I only had six minutes for the download, but I have two patient names that are part of the T-6 Lazarus Project—they don't exist anymore either.

"Jake, I really don't understand what's going on, but there's more. See these added lines—they multiplied your blood alcohol level by 2.5. This other series of additions added line 56 on the history and physical saying that DeMarco had a pacemaker, and changed the autopsy cause of death to pacemaker malfunction—very slick code alteration. Done by a pro and authorized by a Kovalik, whoever that is."

"Can we get the T-6 records? If we do, we can prove my innocence. We can take it to the top. We have it all on paper," said Jake.

"Two major problems, Jake," responded Val, rubbing her eyes. "The actual documents have been transferred to an off-line storage drive—that's what T-6 JUKEBOX means. It's in the T-6 control room but cannot be accessed on the network. The original was erased."

"I can get back in, Val. Just tell me what to do and I'll get the disks."

"That's the least of your problems," answered Val with greater agitation. "Look at this printout, Jake. Do you see the words "BLACKICE" under "BACKUP"? That's the NSA code for the Pentagon and the highest level of security. They're in on it, Jake. Dad was right. This is a spook operation!

"Anyway, Jake, we have to get back to basics here. You did something with your experiment which sparked the Walter Reed brass. The NSC and Pentagon don't get involved unless this thing is either a matter of national security or extreme military concern.

"I have to get to work today and clean up some projects I put on the back burner when Dad died. Against my better judgment, I'm getting involved with you again—not for you but for Dad. For some reason, I still hate government cover-ups. Especially when they hurt innocent individuals—even you!

"Get your act together, stop pitying yourself, and tell me everything that happened. The stuff Dad wrote about in his journal is too unbelievable," she added.

Jake knew that she still carried a lot of baggage and that only time would help. He also knew that he needed Val's help. He remembered her father's very words—"Don't let my daughter get away."

There was nobody else. Besides, her deeply penetrating eyes again reminded him of the only woman he ever regretted treating the way he did. She was actually lovelier than he had ever remembered.

Val got to work at 8 am, leaving Jake in her apartment surrounded by four computers and an incredible mess. First things first—Jake called his commanding officer at the VA Hospital and told him he was sick. He then started looking around the apartment and decided that first he had to clean up and then he had to start thinking about his experiment. What really happened? What combination of events destroyed his career and life?

In the months following his court martial, he had developed writer's block. He refused to think about what happened that fateful night in the T-6 magnet. Val's question was valid. If he expected help or at least some form of cooperation, he had to figure out what could have happened during the experiment to account for the ensuring facts.

7

THE PHYSICS OF METAPHYSICS

THINKING OF THE sequence leading to the MRI accident, Jake believed that the only way he could even start answering questions was by exploring the results of his unearthly experiment. He found a pad and started jotting notes furiously, as if he were writing a scientific paper, but starting with the conclusion. His background in mechanics and quantum physics helped—at least what he remembered.

In reality, much scientific research is written up this way—more than the lay public will ever know. Jake mockingly called this "incidence by coincidence" and had written many skilled articles using this methodology. Part of this he had already written up and handed to Kovalik, but now he needed more:

CONCLUSION:

At 6 Tesla in an experimental MRI, a cancer-riddled female is discovered not only cured of all disease, but also metabolically possessing the constitution of a woman ten years younger.

An elderly male who was in physical contact with the female died and on outward appearance has the physical lesions associated with diffuse cancer.

The government takes over the project and I'm screwed!

PROCEDURE:

The female is placed into the most powerful magnet in the world and is accidentally left in for 2 hours.

An experimental new pulse sequence is applied. This pulse sequence was shown to slow tumor growth on less powerful magnets.

The female was in physical contact with a healthy male throughout the scan.

POSSIBLE HYPOTHESIS:
The "life force" or something resembling an "energy" force was transferred from one person to another—remember Sherlock!

CAUSES OF TRANSFER: refer to 2 variables—high magnetic field and my new experimental pulse—an obvious unknown interaction occurred.

Since ultra-high magnetic fields have been in use at other sites and with other applications, the induction of a new pulse must be the key variable.

All experimental interactions in a magnetic field can and must be explained by Einstein's theory of relativity where $E = mc^2$. Alternatively all equations governing RF pulse frequency are deeply rooted in quantum physics. Physics cannot be changed!

Einstein spent the last 30 years of his life attempting to unify relativity with quantum physics, but I remember an equation replacing electromagnetic frequency and eventually magnetic flux itself for "E" in Einstein's equations.

THAT'S IT! I redefined the equation. My new IR electromagnetic pulse entered a magnetic field 350,000 times the magnetic pull of the earth. Could I have created a "relative black hole" and then placed my pulse into the equation as an unknown variable?

CRITICAL QUESTIONS:
What happens to a quantum of energy when it enters a gravity well of a black hole? Einstein clearly predicted two things. First, it behaves like matter and gets sucked into the central vortex of the field, also known as the "event horizon."

Einstein then defined that once in the event horizon, space and time not only get warped, but also time begins to stretch and our dimensional reference changes. Einstein spoke of a five-dimensional universe. Have I accidentally opened a path to the fifth dimension?

What happened to Sergeant DeMarco? He was within the magnet's most powerful field of influence. Anything within six feet would naturally act as if it were just outside the event horizon of the magnet. Using this theory, Mrs. DeMarco was within the black hole and the sergeant was just outside the event horizon. Something was pulled out of him and into her—WHAT?

CONCLUSION:
All phenomena have to be explained by rules of nature. Something happened in that lab which was not intended in this world or in this dimension.

The key to solving this problem may be the key to understanding the nature of life. SHOULD WE?

Jake reread his notes at least twenty times, each time coming up with an emptier feeling inside. One thing bothered him deeply. He could accept the physics, but the human factor was inexplicable. Jake had never been a very religious youth. His name—"Eriksson"—sounded so noble. Most people had no idea that his great grandfather, a Hungarian Jew, immigrated to America and changed his name from Benjamin Erik Sohnnenheim to Eriksson. His father was a Reform Jew at best. Religion was not Jake's strong point even as an adult. This entry into the metaphysical was very uncomfortable for him. Jake was not even sure he believed in God. He certainly had an even harder time with Heaven and Hell and "spiritual transfer."

For a doctor, Jake tended to eat like a pig. His idea of a low-cholesterol diet usually included three eggs and bacon. Luckily, that's about all Val had in her refrigerator, but it suited him perfectly. It was always easier to think on a full stomach.

He suddenly remembered something he read during his neurology fellowship that struck him as unusual and vaguely applicable to death and the spiritual world. Jake had an almost photographic memory!

"That's it," he mumbled to himself. "EEG analysis of death and dying, an article written by a British neurologist and discredited by the scientific community. I have to track it down!"

EEG stands for electroencephalography, or brain wave analysis. All neurologists are expected to have a basic working knowledge of the external waves generated by the brain and recorded on very sensitive radio receivers implanted on the scalp. Jake, however, took six months off from Harvard and studied EEG interpretation under one of its originators in Oxford. He read almost every article published on the topic. Since most EEGs are utilized for the diagnosis of seizure activity or brain death, much literature was dedicated to those topics. The specific article Jake remembered was the kind that the scientific community is most uncomfortable with—the mixture of science and religion.

It only took thirty minutes on the Internet to find the article. He printed it out from the Medline database. The article was quite well-written and actually published in the *Annals of Neurology*. It was the last article Dr. John Hershberg would ever publish.

It was entitled "Electroencephalographic Proof of the Existence of the Human Spirit." Jake remembered the experiment well, but had never quite read the whole article. It assumed new meaning in light of what had happened.

The experiment was simple. Dr. Hershberg, in the earliest days of EEG research, performed studies on patients during the act of dying. His observations were concise and indisputable. In over one hundred patients, he proved that the EEG recordings continued for over three minutes after all cardiac activity stopped. He also mapped a characteristic EEG voltage spike that preceded a slowly tapering wave. He called the tapering portion of the EEG wave the "lifting" and named the characteristic EEG spike the "God spike." Dr. Hershberg then went one step further and duplicated the experiment in a dog model.

On inducing painless death using potassium chloride lethal injection, however, no God spike or lifting waveform occurred. His conclusion was that a "spiritual essence" was needed and dogs do not have the essence. The simple experiment would have been characterized as one of the leading articles in the *Annals*, except for one thing. Dr. Hershberg was a devout Orthodox Jew and the concluding paragraph in his paper referred to this experiment as the "sine qua non proof of the existence of God and a spiritual life after death in man alone."

Although the work was impeccable, western science and religion never melded well. Dr. Hershberg was denied tenure at the University of Chicago and could never find another academic job. Rumor has it that he became an Orthodox rabbi and one of Europe's leading experts in Kabalistic Judaism, the mystical and often taboo study of Judaic numerology and nontraditional spells and spiritualism. In a remote biblical reference, it is stated that Kabalistic experiments have brought the dead to life and even unleashed undead creatures called "Golems." In the books of the Kabala, only the most learned and sophisticated rabbis could achieve such feats, and only by becoming literally one with the lower essence of God. Dr. Hershberg was rumored to have created life by Kabalistic incantations during his later studies; however, such things are not talked about. Jake may have discovered a shortcut.

In the meantime, Hershberg's experiment was never confirmed and seven editorials in the *Annals of Neurology* refuted the experiment on the ground of faulty EEG interpretation.

Although the article was officially withdrawn from publication, many neurology fellows knew of its content and often joked around about the God spike in EEGs. It was the kind of black humor thing doctors were famous for, but Jake always wondered.

The article downloaded from the Internet contained the entire experiment. To Jake's surprise, it also contained detailed examples of the waveforms of the God spike as well as the lifting.

He had to get his data back from Walter Reed. He had to break into the T-6 scanner. He needed the EEGs of all of the patients that were experimented on for comparison.

Val's day at the NSC was no less disturbing. After nearly no sleep and the most unusual revelations in her computer career, many emotional issues bothered her. Things change over the years. Both she and Jake were so idealistic at Harvard. So in love. Now he lay in her apartment, destroyed by an obvious government operation. The code on the cover-up program was "BlackIce." How could she ever tell Jake that BlackIce was written entirely by her? They were using her brains to destroy him. She never really looked into herself. Her soul was now as black as the programs she was writing for the government. Like a bomber dropping lethal bombs from 20,000 feet, Val was writing spook code for the government and breaking into programs that eventually led to people getting killed. Interventions leading to governments toppling. Secret operations run by government agencies that even the President of the United States did not know about.

Colonel Richardson interrupted her thoughts. "Val, you look like you haven't slept for weeks. Are you okay?"

"I'm all right, Colonel. I'm still getting over my father's death." Her mind, however, was actively planning the next move. She was committed to finding the truth at all costs—for her father's sake.

"Listen, Val, take some more time off. I'll do the paper-work."

"Colonel, the best medicine for me is work right now," responded Val quickly. She needed an entry to the Walter Reed mainframe computer, and this was it.

"I just found a possible level one breach at Walter Reed during my standard intrusion search. It's probably nothing but one of your boys getting out on the net and downloading some dirty pictures of teenage cheerleaders. Let me go into the field and investigate it. I think getting my hands dirty with a small detective project like this is what the doctor ordered."

"You got it, Val," answered Richardson with a grin. "You find that son of a bitch and we'll throw the book at him!"

Val returned to her apartment with a well-formulated plan. She needed to download the information about Project Lazarus, and the only way was by getting to the T-6 remote archive computer. Her quick thinking gave her complete access to Walter Reed. The colonel immediately cleared her way for a full breach investigation with top-secret security clearance. The "game was afoot," as Sherlock Holmes would have said.

She was shocked when she walked into her apartment. The lights were dimmed, a lovely fire burning, and the aroma of veal saltimbocca, her favorite Italian meal.

"Jake, you'll make someone a great wife," Val smiled on seeing him hover over the stove in a silly flowered apron.

"Just wanted to thank you for dragging me in last night, Val," he responded with a soft smile. "We have a lot to talk about. Might as well do it over a nice meal and a bottle of Merlot. I did some research on the Net, both medical and nonmedical."

"I did a little work myself, Jake," replied Val. "I'm going into Walter Reed tomorrow afternoon. You have to describe the T-6 lab to me so that I can get in and out of the remote computer without much attention. I faked a computer breach. If they leave me alone for five minutes, I can download the entire database."

"That's great. Once we have the data, we can get attention. Val, I started developing a theory of what happened, but it's all so crazy! I wrote some of the stuff down. We can talk about it after dinner. I started thinking about some of the strange things that I have seen in medicine and some of the stuff we learned in physics at Harvard. Somehow, I think I managed to bridge the gap. I'm not sure I can convince you of anything yet, Val. Most of the stuff I'm hypothesizing sounds crazy even to me and I witnessed the experiment myself."

"You're not crazy, Jake," answered Val. "The files I uncovered all indicated one thing. The brass and spooks all consider your project TOP SECRET. "BlackIce" was the code word and I wrote the security programming that allowed them to fake all of your documents. I don't know how to say this, but they used my code to destroy you, and probably a hell of a lot of other people. It's nearly undetectable and used for only limited projects. This thing is real."

"What did Shakespeare say—there is no more dangerous creature than a woman scorned?" responded Jake.

"Something like that, Jake. Your physics is probably better than your Bard," smiled Val.

After dinner, Val read the notes Jake had jotted down with not only interest but an almost intuitive feel for the evolving theory. She had studied Einstein's theory of relativity in far greater depth than Jake had. The black hole concept of magnetic fields and time/dimension theory always fascinated her. She even attended some fascinating seminars in D.C. by a very eccentric Nobel Prize laureate named Abernathy Jones.

The interesting thing was not that Professor Jones had won the Nobel Prize for unifying quantum physics and relativity. He had proved mathematically that the interactions of two black holes might be described as harmonics similar to strings, called unified string theory. The interesting thing was that Dr. Jones was one of the foremost experts of the paranormal in the world.

Physics and ghosts don't normally mix in the same academic circles, but the President of Georgetown University tolerated Dr. Jones. So Jones used his sabbaticals to hunt ghosts in Scotland using sophisticated instruments designed for jungle warfare and magnetic physics. So he was featured on the Discovery Channel as the "Ghost Doctor." The President had no problems with innocent eccentricities. If only the Board of Directors felt the same way!

The following morning they both sat in on the colloquia normally held by the Department of Physics of Georgetown. It was in Reiss 502. The schedule was on the Department of Physics web page, and colloquia were generally open to the public—not that a lecture by Professor Jones on superconductivity and field theory was a standing room only event.

Dr. Jones wore a wrinkled brown tweed jacket with dark brown corduroy pants. He spoke with a slow, deliberate voice and had a very pleasant, somewhat subdued demeanor. He would sometimes stop in mid-sentence, as if he had lost his train of thought. Or perhaps at that moment he was unraveling the secrets of the universe. It was hard to tell. His students loved him, especially when he would occasionally digress into the paranormal. Jake and Val sat quietly in the back holding a legal satchel filled with notes and papers.

The end of the lecture was Jake and Val's chance. Perhaps Jones could help tie things together. Very few people understood both physics and the paranormal.

"Professor Jones!" yelled Val in the hallway as he exited the classroom. "We're sorry to disturb you, but do you have a moment?"

"Are you reporters or TV people looking to make fun of an eccentric old physics professor?" asked Jones.

"No, professor," interjected Jake. "If anything, we want absolutely no publicity. I'm a doctor specializing in neurology and magnetic field research. We may have discovered something unexplainable by medical science or physics. I'm in trouble. I'm not sure anyone can help but if you can just listen for a few minutes—"

Jake did not finish his sentence. Abernathy Jones may have had a few years behind him and may have been called a lunatic by more than one colleague, but he possessed a keen eye and sense of the truth. He could spot a liar a mile away. Most ghost sightings were nothing more than bullshit.

"Come to my office," he responded with a wave of his hand.

The next two hours were spent recounting every detail of the T-6 experiment, reviewing Jake's notes on his theories of the experiment, and reading and rereading Dr. Hershberg's theories on EEG patterns during death and the "proof" of existence of the human spirit. Jones was actually most fascinated by the Hershberg paper. He thought he knew of every paper published on the spiritual world. How could he have overlooked this landmark study?

After a barrage of probing questions, Jones spent another twenty minutes looking at the data and reading the papers, not saying a word. Jake and Val just looked at each other. Their unspoken words said the same thing: maybe this was a mistake.

When Jones finally broke the oppressive silence, his words were simple and to the point.

"Doctor Eriksson, I have won the Nobel Prize in quantum physics. I studied under Guggenheim and redefined the glorious equations you quite adeptly refer to in your notes. I have seen with my own eyes spirits in Scottish castles. I have recorded the electromagnetic flux of the spiritual energy of the dead. You, however, have done what no mortal should ever have the power to do. You are playing God, and I will have nothing to do with this unholy experiment. If the government is involved, they must be stopped. That is your business and I will have nothing to do with it."

This was not the expected response. Both Jake and Val had hoped Dr. Jones would be sparked by the evidence, not turned off. They were flabbergasted.

"Is it that something doesn't make sense—is that it?" asked Val with a confused look on her face.

Dr. Jones gently smiled and replied, "No, my child, it is that for the first time in my life I truly do understand. You may have unified the theories of physics and metaphysics. You have accidentally melded Einstein's theory of black holes with what Dr. Hershberg called the 'lifting.' It is under your nose, yet you do not see it. You have discovered the 'God pulse'! Your new pulse sequence—check the records. I guarantee that your patient's EEG will demonstrate what you call the characteristic 'God spike.' The high magnetic field acts as a facilitator and a vector.

"You see, all of my investigations have led me to one conclusion. Spirits *must* obey the same laws of relativistic and quantum physics that exist for all matter and antimatter. That means that when in the center of your so-called MRI fake black hole, you have caused the 'lifting' of one spirit *into* the vortex of the quantum singularity. You have replaced it with the 'soul' and remaining life force energy of the body just outside the black hole—the magnet pulls in life energy and deposits it into another body once the God pulse ceases."

"But what happens to the soul of the body inside the black hole, and what happens to consciousness?" asked Jake.

"Even Einstein could only speculate on what exists on the other side of a black hole. Is it another dimension, is it heaven, or is it hell? Dr. Eriksson, you are liberating souls into an abyss not intended to be explored by mortals such as we. I have always been a scientist. Our most sacred rule is observe, record, but do not disrupt that which we do not understand. Please leave now. I shall have nothing more to do with this! You have broken our most sacred rule. You have disrupted and interfered without understanding, and now the government is probably performing even greater abominations."

And that was their last contact with Professor Abernathy Jones. He retired the following month, and left no forwarding address. It was announced in the *Washington Post*.

This interaction only heightened Jake and Val's sense of what needed to be done. They needed to get the evidence out of the T-6 lab.

In a dark office two miles underneath the Pentagon, General Richard Drew of the top-secret Plasma Weapons Division sat behind his stark desk.

"What brings you to the bowels of the Pentagon at this late hour, Abernathy?" asked Drew.

"Richard, we have known each other for what—ten years? Not many Pentagon projects have Nobel Prize winners on their staff." That statement always had an ominous meaning to the general. It meant he was about to be popped for a favor.

"I know you long enough to discern when you want something from me," replied Drew with his usual expressionless military voice. He rustled some papers on his desk, looking up only occasionally.

Jones rarely asked for much, but when he did it was usually a pain in the ass for the Pentagon—like getting him permission to set up ghost-busting equipment in that silly Scottish castle. Nonetheless, his job was to keep Jones happy until the plasma gun project was completed, and that was not to be for a while. Jones's particle theories were integral in perfecting the first weapon of mass destruction fully functional in zero gravity. These were guns with small matter/antimatter reactors shooting a burst of plasma capable of vaporizing a tank in a millisecond. Talk about a Pentagon dream! Drew never understood how they got Jones to cooperate.

"This one's easy, Richard," responded Jones with a blank look in his eyes. "I want access to Project Lazarus. No questions on how or what I know—just give me full Pentagon security access."

Back above ground, Val's appointment at Walter Reed was at 1300 hours. She reported to General Paul Kovalik's office promptly. Val was never one to flaunt her figure, but this project needed every distraction at her disposal. Her dress was a little too short and her blouse a little too open for military spec. Few military men could ignore the curves this highway had!

As she entered General Kovalik's office, she mumbled her favorite Mae West quote to herself—"It's better to be looked over than overlooked!"

"Very pleased to meet you, Miss—Wright, is it?" smiled Kovalik with a quick glance at Val's cleavage line. "This dog can still hunt," he thought to himself. "I just wouldn't know what to do once I caught it!"

"General Kovalik, as you know, I am director of the cryptography division of the NSA and I wrote all of your security encryption," responded Val with a professional tone. "A routine sweep with a detection program called a 'hunter probe' detected several lost links in your T-6 project computer. It's probably nothing more than a corrupt program, but as you know, we have a BlackIce label on the T-6 project and all alerts are taken *very* seriously."

"You have our cooperation," responded Kovalik. "The Colonel called ahead and said you were the best. We stopped all experiments effective 1100 hours. The lab is yours. Doctor Sam Smith, project leader, will accompany you."

"Thank you very much, General, but other than showing me the way, I would hate to have Dr. Smith inconvenienced for two hours while I perform a routine anti-incursion sweep," interjected Val, a little more quickly than she meant to. Any attention, and especially another person in the room, would prevent her from downloading the research data from the offline server.

"Now, Miss Wright, if you wrote the program and probably the security regulations, you know the rules on BlackIce. Any officer or security personnel may operate BlackIce computers only in the presence of another BlackIce cleared operative. Doctor Smith will just have to suffer being around you for two hours," he said with a sheepish smile. "You wouldn't be trying to get me into trouble?"

Val glanced at the picture of the President and General Kovalik on the wall just as Doctor Smith entered the office. "No, General," she smiled. "I don't think little ol' me can do that, sir."

Doctor Smith escorted Val to the T-6 suite. The subbasement of Walter Reed was not quite what she had expected. The entire wing looked freshly redesigned. Video monitors in every hallway with one entry point guard by the elevator and three smart-card access terminals leading to the final hallway. Her BlackIce clearance card was needed at all doors.

Once in the T-6 console room, Val's eyes stared at the unit with amazement. The front console room was separated from the magnet by a translucent glittering gold mesh wall forming a shield around the high magnetic field. The magnet was the size of a small trailer home. It had three claw-like wedge-shaped components with a funneled rear. The claws were open. In the rear was a circular disk with two rows of lights slowly pulsating in opposite directions. A plastic acrylic stretcher sat in the center of the magnet's claws. A second stretcher sat at a 90-degree angle to the first. Binding restraints for arms and legs were evident on both stretchers.

A rhythmic, low-pitched hum permeated the room. The pulse echoed Val's heartbeat at about sixty cycles per second.

The control room looked like mission control at NASA. Rows of monitors and full studio video equipment were positioned in full view of the scanner room. The control console had monitors clearly labeled ECG, EEG, pulse oximiter, and BP. To the right of the control console, Val saw a separate computer labeled Backup Server. The optical storage disk drive was immediately to the right of the monitor. Smith saw the look in her eyes. "Quite a sight," commented Smith.

"Excuse me?" replied Val, slightly startled. Her mind was working on a plan to get to the backup server. She needed to download all of the research data without being observed. "I was looking at the scanner. My dad had several MRI's at the Baltimore VA, but those scanners looked nothing like what you have here."

"That's because the scanners at the VA are 1.5 Tesla. This scanner runs at 6 Tesla. The magnet is so powerful that when activated, it can literally take even the trace fibers in your clothing and suck them into the bore of the unit. It can crush you like a grape. That's why patients have to wear paper gowns especially made with an anti-paramagnetic coating. We recently made special paper gowns for the technologists, which actually look like regular clothing. At first we tried to get them to wear the patient gowns, but the rear opening bothered them," winked Smith.

"Oh, you doctors," sighed Val in her girlish sexy voice. "You're all such cads!" She muttered "what a dork" under her breath. But this was war. Theft of government secrets to aid a military felon under general court-martial orders won't look pretty on her record. Maybe leading Doctor Dork into thinking he's going to get to first base would act as a decoy. "Doctor Smith, I hate to think that I am wasting your valuable time. I have about two hours of work here and I am perfectly comfortable. You can come back if you have some other work to do."

"I'm afraid I cannot do that, Ms. Wright," responded Smith. "Your security division makes up all the rules. Article

58 clearly states that 'no BlackIce security site shall allow unaccompanied visitors regardless of rank and/or security clearance.'"

Good try, thought Val. It was difficult for her to hide her disappointment. Maybe she had overdone it with the cute routine. The asshole probably wanted to hang around her longer, she thought. Nonetheless, she opened up her briefcase and pulled out three diagnostic diskettes then plugged her laptop into the mainframe.

The rest was routine. Complete virus checks as well as intruder sniffers. They ran by themselves, but Val could do some online exploration even while being watched. Smith's eyes were never off her.

Once she was finished with the mainframe, she drifted toward the right to start the same process on the backup drive.

"Ms. Wright, that drive simply serves as a backup and there is no access to it via the network. There is no need for you to interrogate it," stated Smith with a somewhat harsh tone.

"I'm aware of your network architecture," responded Val with a similar official tone. "I hope you are aware that my clearance actually supersedes yours and that this lab may have had an unauthorized computer breach. Your download records show that all information is immediately backed to two servers, one of which is here and the other in a remote site. Your need to then destroy the primary information is your business, sir. As long as one bit of information is down-loaded to this backup archive, I am responsible for ensuring the safety of this information. Last year a Pentagon breach introduced a virus that contaminated all archive and backup devices. We blew it at first because we only decontaminated the mainframe. A small computer acting as a router was actually missed and reintroduced the virus with significant consequences. I'm not making a similar mistake."

Smith sat down and smiled. Val got the distinct feeling that Smith was suspicious of her. She was right. As she started working on the archive she glanced at the directory, trying to memorize as much as she could. The directory held all of the index information for the entire backup archive. It was something like trying to memorize the fifteen-volume *Encyclopedia Britannica* index as it flashed across a computer screen at 100 pages per minute.

Smith was on her like a cheap Italian suit. Her chances of downloading the research data files were nonexistent. Val just finished up and left, noting the exact location of the doors, locks, and guards. She also noticed the configuration of the entry passes. They were Pentagon vintage. She could use her own pass, but her code would be immediately detected on the morning incursion sweep. Any attempted reentry would be a one-way ticket for her career—one way to the state pen!

8

TRIAL OF THE REVEREND

FAIRFAX COUNTY, VIRGINIA, 19th Judicial Court, was the site of what many dubbed the trial of the century. By all written accounts, the Reverend Morten Dublaise has committed more murders than Ted Bundy. The main difference between the two was that Dublaise had a following that was not only well armed, but had connections that infiltrated the highest levels of the government. His preaching of a "New World Order" appealed to an incredible number of individuals. Any government intervention reminded the liberal separatist and white supremacist groups of Ruby Ridge and the department of Alcohol, Tobacco, and Firearms screwup.

The actual crimes of Dublaise were ignored by many, and his trial became the fulcrum for every antigovernment group in the nation. The scene was reminiscent of the OJ trial. The anti-abortionists, separatists, skinheads, neo-Nazis, and even some radical wings of the Republican Party gathered to petition for the release of the Reverend. "He was framed because of his opinions," was the outcry of his followers. "Hitler had it right all along. He just didn't finish the job! This country has been sold to the niggers and Jews."

As the trial progressed, more and more fringe groups aligned themselves with the Dublaise cult. The scene outside of the courthouse was chaotic. Midnight vigils, cult members distributing propaganda, and threats of mass retaliation if Dublaise was convicted. Armed police and FBI officers were on constant watch. CNN broadcasts invariably focused on young men and women being dragged to the lockup because of disorderly conduct. The Vietnam protests were the last time this country was so focused on anti-government protests and riots.

Things were nearly as chaotic inside the courthouse. Judge Wilhelmina Jackson presided. She was black, a fact that infuriated the Dublaise cult members and drew comments from even the liberal press. Getting control inside the courtroom was as difficult as preventing a riot outside the courtroom. Judge Jackson, however, was a tough magistrate and would tolerate no disruption in her Federal Court.

The introductory presentations by the defense and prosecuting attorneys were the usual rhetoric. The jury even showed signs of boredom — until the prosecution presented the visual and forensic evidence.

The Dublaise path was riddled with death. FBI investigations of his early parishes profiled a classic serial killer. A quiet, somewhat unassuming man with a hidden passion only brought to the surface by his captivating sermons. His piercing blue eyes with an almost hypnotic appeal. A soft-spoken voice, capable of subtle inflections and volume shifts that pierced the listener's heart.

His killing pattern was similar in every instance. A slow start, somewhat uncharacteristic for a Baptist minister. As familiarity slipped in, the sermons became stronger. The inner rage slowly awakened, as if a different and possessed individual came to life.

In each parish, Dublaise initiated a youth group dedicated to community service. His grip was strong and his demands were often overbearing, but the parents of the children unanimously showed approval and support. He used Hitler's techniques in unifying the youth first as a template.

"It's about time the church supported strong moral standards," they would unanimously say. The Reverend was a missionary, and missionaries preaching the word of the Lord needed to be given latitude.

Toward the end of each tenure, however, Dublaise's dark side always emerged. The sleeper awakened and the results were always the same. A young woman mysteriously disappeared. In and of itself, the events had no unusual pattern in our culture. Abductions, killings, and rapes are a sign of our times, even in the remotest of towns. Young teenage boys opening up automatic weapons and wiping out their class members classically occur in little towns in Kansas. Only when the entire picture was presented would the jury see the path of devastation.

The photographs shown by the prosecution would make even a coroner ill. The FBI tracked down hidden graves in nearly every parish Dublaise presided over. Photographs of dismembered bodies, burned skeletons, and indisputable dental records brought tears and shouts of agony from the victims' family members.

The courtroom was filled with families victimized by Dublaise. Many have lived with the hope that their little girls would come back, that they had just run away from home. In front of them lay two revelations, the final chapter in the story of their children and indisputable evidence pointing to the Reverend Morten Dublaise.

As the prosecution worked its way through the evidence, the accounts became more graphic and the evidence better preserved. Like most serial killers, Dublaise became more brazen in his acts as time went by. He covered his tracks less efficiently, leaving clear-cut evidence.

Bodies were discovered in shallow graves. One body disposed of in the Susquehanna River actually floated to the surface and into a local tributary, where a dog sniffed it out. Forensic evidence of Dublaise's semen, hair, DNA, and skin samples taken from the pretty young blonde's finger-nails told the story of a brutal rape and murder. The only thing not recognizable was her face, brutally pummeled by a semi-blunt object. The coroner found the pickaxe with trace blood on the spade in the church shed behind the parish Dublaise shepherded. The blood type and DNA matched perfectly.

During the trial, Dublaise sat silently. Although he wore a prison shirt and khaki slacks, his nervous habit endured. A continuous rubbing of his neck, right forefinger inside his collar—as if his phantom priest's collar remained. No remorse, no kindness, and no sadness. He had that Charlie Manson look that pierced the hearts and souls of all who gazed at him. At times he mumbled under his breath and then smiled. Several who sat next to him swore they could hear the name "Clarice" before his occasional smiles. They had no idea what that meant.

"You'll all burn in hell!" shouted a woman, Dublaise follower, in back of the courtroom. "For the Lord shall lead the heathen into the depths of hell, and the lord is Jehovah, and he shall return as the Messiah. Heed the words of the Messiah, for he is here amongst us—he is amongst us!"

As the marshals forcibly escorted the woman from the courtroom, shouts came from all corners of the courtroom. "You are condemning the Christ! You all follow the footsteps of Judas! Jews and niggers, all of you—Jews and niggers!"

"Clear the courtroom, bailiff—immediately!" shouted Judge Jackson, smashing her gavel onto the desk. "Clear the courtroom!"

The remainder of the trial was held in a courtroom free of spectators. Only the victims' families remained. The trial was closed circuit televised to an outside observation room and then to the world via a network television link. The morbidly curious were glued to their television sets. Network commentary was incessant. Self-proclaimed legal experts and anyone with even a remote history of involvement with an interesting murder trial would make a small fortune in the ensuing weeks. Tabloid justice.

Despite the protests, defense pleas for a mistrial, and the challenges to the validity of the forensic evidence, the jury verdict was unanimous: guilty on all counts. Kidnapping, twenty-five counts of premeditated murder, twelve counts of cult activity, and a myriad of local and federal charges. Not the least of the charges included a variety of weapons and explosives posessions as well as federal theft of nuclear explosive plans and raw radioactive materials from Fort Bragg.

"Your honor," spoke Dublaise in a calm yet deeply penetrating voice. "Prior to judgment, I would like to invoke my privilege and make a statement in my defense. I would like to especially address the families of my victims."

"You have five minutes and not one second more," responded Judge Jackson. "I am showing you far greater latitude than you have shown your victims."

"Thank you, your honor," started Dublaise, slowly rubbing the inside of his collar. "As God asked Abraham to sacrifice his only son. As God led Moses out of the desert and into the Holy Land. As God made Jesus His son and resurrected him from the dead, so has God spoken to me, for I am the Messiah. I have killed nobody, for liberation of the mortal soul is my greatest gift to mankind. Those reaped in the early harvest shall be my prophets and my saints, for they led me to the lessons God wanted me to learn."

Tears and sobbing came from the few remaining families allowed to witness the judgment.

"Cry not, my flock! We have all sinned and God has made me his avatar. We shall all soon join in the heavens. My holy army shall avenge the Father, the Son, and the Holy Spirit, for I am all—I am one with the Lord, and the Lord shall have mercy only on his flock—I shall return as Lazarus returned and destroy the unbelievers—"

"I've heard enough!" shouted the judge.

But Dublaise's volume and fervor increased. His eyes were like open flames and he was not to be stopped. His hands rose to the heavens, shouting, "I shall return stronger than ever and all my followers shall know my sign. As is written in the Old Testament, my name shall be Hashem—I shall return!"

They were the last words of Morten Dublaise. As the bailiff forcibly removed him from the court, Judge Jackson retired to her chamber to decide the sentence.

By the Nielsen ratings, an incredible 72 percent of people watching television were tuned into the trial at 5:45. Jake and Val were tuned into CNN, interrupting their review of the day's futile events to see the verdict in the trial of the century.

Judge Jackson was brief. "There are few decisions harder to make as a judge than sending a man to his death. In this case, however, my heart and conscience are clear. The prosecution proved its case beyond any reasonable doubt. In his early years, Reverend Morten Dublaise, under the guise of a man of the cloth, brutally molested and murdered at least six women. Charges of kidnapping, federal bombing, mass murder related to cult activity, federal arms charges, nuclear isotope theft, and continued cult activity clearly seen even outside of this courtroom lead me to believe that anything less than the death sentence will pose a continued threat to society. I hereby sentence Morten Dublaise to death by lethal injection and refuse any motion for appeal."

"What a sick bastard," commented Jake. "And to think the son of a bitch was building a nuclear bomb. Guess he wanted to pull a Noah—wipe the earth clear and start anew."

"Well, I'm glad at least he's one less thing the world has to worry about, Jake," responded Val. "We, on the other hand, have one shitload of a problem! I have to get back inside—but this time after hours."

"Val, you risked your career for me already. I can't ask for more. I'll get in and download the information—just tell

me what to do. This is it for me, Val. If I don't show up at the
VA tomorrow, I'm AWOL and Kovalik will throw the book at
me. This is my game now and I have to finish it. You can't get
involved."

Val's eyes were ablaze. "Jake, you still don't understand,
do you? This is a BlackIce spook operation. You have no place
to turn because everyone who holds the cards is involved. I
wrote the programming and the protocols. Any bad feelings I
have ever had for you aside, I despise what I have become. I am
a tool used by the government. I have lost total control of my
projects—a far cry from my idealistic days at MIT. Professor
Romanoff was right. I should never have gotten involved with
the NSA. Jake, I'm the only one that can help you, and you
are doing *nothing* without me. Do you understand? These are
my rules!"

Jake just stared at Val speechlessly. He knew that argument
was futile. He also knew that she was right. Her skills as a
computer programmer and hacker were unmatched. She was
the only one who could get through, but they had to do it
together.

"Let's get working, Val." Jake was uncomfortable with Val
directly involved. A little reconnaissance was one thing, but
actual intrusion into a secure facility—that's Federal Penitentiary material.

"We need entry, Jake. I can use my pass card and write
in some overrides using the pass codes I downloaded from
the server, but the second I put my personal card in, my
hunter-killers will detect an irregularity. They will set up a
trace and report a low-level internal breach within 24 hours
to the commanding officer. These breaches are usually late
shift changes and have no consequences, but I think Smith is
suspicious. Once he sees my name on a security breach, he'll
be on us within minutes."

9

MANNY RODRIGUEZ

"SERGEANT RODRIGUEZ—MRI," answered a male voice with a strong Puerto Rican accent.

"Manny, this is Jake, can you talk?"

"Jake," whispered Manny. "You shouldn't be calling here. I just got a notice from Military Security that you are AWOL—considered armed and dangerous. What kind of shit are you into, buddy? I don't believe any of the stuff they fed us. You're into some high-level screw job!"

"Manny, I know you have a wife and kids—I have nowhere to turn and I need some inside help—I feel guilty as shit about calling, but can we meet?"

Manny responded without a moment's hesitation. "Jake, we're friends. You always treated me good and I hate it when nice guys get screwed. Meet me at Bud's Bar around the corner, next to Shepard Park—and don't call here again!"

Bud's was the local military strip joint. The brass never showed up in such an inappropriate establishment, but most of the enlisted men loved the burgers and beer—not to mention the lovely college girls trying to earn their tuition by tips. The place was an ideal meeting place, and they picked a dark corner behind the bar. Most of the men were facing the other way, watching the entertainment. Their conversation was low nonetheless.

"Jake, once that sergeant died in the scanner and you were blamed for his death, I knew that it was all a bunch of bullshit. That guy never had a pacer. I did the preliminary workup for you, don't you remember? I told the CO, but he told me that this was top secret stuff and I ought to mind my own business. Then it became a black military operation and all of us were taken off the T-6 project—except for Carlson, that bitch! I told you she would get you into trouble, Captain. Always thinking with your dick!"

"I know everything, Manny. I got access to the T-6 main-frame, but I have no proof—gotta get the records out of the mainframe backup. That's why I need your help. I need two things. I need you to track the address and phone number of Mrs. DeMarco, the sergeant's wife. She's gone and I can't trace her."

"No problema."

"Then I need a Level 1 security badge to breach the T-6 compound. I also need the patrol schedule of the T-6 lab security guards."

"Un problema grande, amigo," sighed Manny. "Us fat Puerto Ricans look very bad in stripes. Makes us look even fatter. Then again—we meet here in two days, O.K.?"

As in most military facilities, the system was run by relatively low-level personnel, all operating on a need-to-know basis. Manny had many favors owed him in Walter Reed. He covered his tracks adeptly. Each of his friends executed a task without any knowledge of the final chain or outcome. Nothing was traceable to Manny. The blank ID card disappeared from central supply while Manny was picking up a case of barium for the main X-ray department. Although the cards were numbered, he picked the last in the batch. At best, this would be picked up next year, and probably never, since it would be attributed to a random counting error.

Programming the card took a little more effort. He tracked down the access list for the T-6 project and found a computer subcontractor whose pass expired. Manny went through the official paperwork and hand-carried a request for his reactivation to the security office. The photograph ID code, however, was Jake's old code, which still resided on the mainframe. Manny knew almost everyone in security.

"Hi, Linda, how's it shaking, mamacita?" asked Manny with his best horny grin.

"Listen, Emanuel," replied Linda Esperanza, the security duty officer. "If you're not careful, I'll tell your wife on you and she'll do what any Latino wife should with a husband like you—cut your balls off!"

"You hurt me, Linda. Anyway, those three-stripe ass-holes have me running secretary duty now. I got this badge to reactivate for T-6. Some computer nerd they need to fix something."

Although slightly distracted, Linda performed the appropriate background check. Manny was afraid that the picture of Jake would not match the description—but it was close enough for Linda not to notice the slight difference in eye color.

"You know, Manny, these L1 badges are only given in person. I am breaking regulations and you owe me. I'll do it for you just in case I get lonely one night."

"I will ruin it for every other man that makes love to you, mamacita," grinned Manny, holding the Level 1 T-6 clearance ID with Jake's picture.

The patrol schedule was much easier to get. Manny's first cousin Roberto worked the graveyard security detail. Manny knew the combination of his locker. Roberto was a first cousin on his mother's side—the stupid side of the family. It took him a month to memorize his telephone number. The patrol schedule was in his uniform pocket as expected, a definite security breach.

The exchange went as planned at Bud's Bar. Manny first sat down and ordered a burger and beer. Jake came in and sat next to him. He sat on a hard object, discreetly reached down, and slipped the envelope left on the chair in his pocket.

Jake thanked Manny by looking at the bar mirror, making eye contact and discreetly nodding his head.

"It never happened, my man," mumbled Manny into his beer. "I still gotta get you that address—meet me in a few."

Back in Val's apartment, intense preparations were under way. Val reviewed all the security pass codes and building layouts one more time. Once in Walter Reed, they had to avoid all cameras. Jake knew every hallway and stairwell in the hospital, but as in most military institutions, secret cameras were everywhere. It was like being in Vegas.

"Jake, your friend Manny really came through. I want you to understand, though, that it is standard operating procedure to reissue access codes randomly."

"What does that mean, Val?"

"It means that if your card stops working, we can't turn back. It means that I use my card and when that happens, every bell and whistle will go off from here to the Pentagon within 24 hours and I won't have a fancy enough explanation to get out of it. It means I'm ready to run the gauntlet if we get caught, Jake."

"I have no option, Val, I'm already running. You can still back out."

Val never responded.

10

RUNNING THE GAUNTLET

WALTER REED ARMY Medical Center was a world-renowned facility. Getting through the front gate at 11:45 was as easy as flashing two Level 1 badges. Both Val and Jake wore basic black underneath somewhat colorful shirts. They wore slightly tinted glasses, not enough to demand attention but just enough to cause off-angle camera reflections. They turned right immediately after entry into the main lobby, heading away from the T-6 elevators and towards the maintenance wing. Jake knew the wing well—it housed all of the on-call rooms.

"We have to get down to sub-basement 3 using the back stairwell. That takes us to the nursing quarters and the back elevator shaft," whispered Jake as he adeptly led them through familiar ground.

"The nurses' quarters—no wonder you seem so at home in these hallways. Bet you can even negotiate them in the dark," responded Val with the requisite annoyance. Jake ignored the remarks, although she was technically correct.

As they rounded the first hallway, they heard voices. Jake glanced at his watch. Twelve o'clock and change of shift.

"Shit, Val. We have to get into one of these rooms." They quickly tried three locked doors in a row only to open the fourth. It was a broom closet with room enough for the broom. They desperately squeezed in. The words "too close for comfort" came to both of their minds. This was, however, no time for modesty. They stood face to face, pressed closely together. Jake could feel Val's firm breasts pressing against his chest. This closeness revived many fond memories . . . he had traveled that road before. "Wrong time . . . " Jake thought.

The voices stopped and they waited about 45 more seconds before cracking the door about two inches. The hallway was clear. They both took off their colorful shirts and dumped them in the broom closet before leaving. They were now dressed in basic black. Once past the final hallway, getting caught meant prison.

The elevator going to the back corridor of T-6 was in front of them. Jack took the patrol schedule out and looked at his watch. Val pulled out a computer schematic of the surveillance camera system of the sub-basement. She got it using a minor computer intrusion into the Federal Architectural Repository. Thank God the government is so anal about its records. They had 37 minutes and a well-rehearsed path. Jake pushed the timer button on his watch. Avoiding camera sweeps meant impeccable timing and NO mistakes!

They made an immediate right once the elevator door opened. They had two security doors to pass through and then the T-6 magnet entry door. As they dodged past the first hallway camera sweeping towards them, Jake jammed the fake ID card into the door switch.

"Work, baby—work," mumbled Jake. The milliseconds seemed to last an eternity.

A three-tone alert flashed a green light on the door panel and the sliding security door opened with a high-pitched hiss. They were in! The second hallway was longer and demanded two moves to avoid the camera. The first move was a straight dart along the left wall to a nurse's station originally intended for patient registration for the magnet. They hid behind the station desk for seven seconds, carefully watching the far camera. Once out of sweep range, they darted along the right wall and activated the second security door, opening it identically as they opened the first.

Once in the T-6 corridor, no surveillance cameras were mounted. The high magnetic field caused too much interference for conventional cameras, and the dedicated magnetically shielded cameras were impractical for wall mounting. This gave them more time, but Jake's countdown was at 32 minutes. The download would take 15 minutes, giving them 17 minutes to get in and out before the security patrol. As scheduled, the officer normally guarding the door was away on patrol.

Jake inserted his fake ID into the T-6 security door, expecting the same opening sequence as with the other two doors. The green light never came. Sweat started accumulating above his upper lip.

"Maybe upside down!" cried Val. Jake immediately reversed the card.

"No go, Princess Leia. I'm afraid you need your Han Solo now!"

"Not really," responded Val with a look of finality. "I just hope they allow communal visits where we're going."

Val had no sooner inserted her personal security card then the door hissed open, green light and all.

She had just played her trump card. Her back door just closed and they had less than 24 hours—that is, if they managed to get out of Walter Reed without getting caught.

The 17 minutes they originally had were now only 10 minutes. This final incursion took precious minutes longer than expected. It was a no-go, the numbers no longer worked for a safe exit.

"Val, we don't have time for the download. We are 7 minutes shy of a clean escape. We have to leave now!" cried Jake with near panic in his voice.

"Like hell," responded Val, jamming the small CD disk into the computer archive and starting the download.

"The guard is coming in 9 minutes, we have 15 minutes of download time. If he sees nothing, we have until the next shift, giving us 27 minutes. The CD backup is silent, so all we have to do is hide."

They both simultaneously looked at the open claws of the gigantic T-6 magnet. Val started shaking her head—"In there?" she asked with a tremulous voice.

"There's nowhere else. The magnet is open, but we can close the gantry and hide inside the bore. The guard will never know since he can't come into the magnetic room with his gun or flashlight. The magnet is almost always stored with closed claws. Take your clothes off!" demanded Jake.

"Why? I have no metal on me."

"Val, trust me, this magnet has 400,000 times the magnetic pull of the Earth. Trace metal elements in clothing will crush you like a grape. We have to strip!"

Jake was already removing his shirt while Val was protesting.

"Now wait, Jake, I heard this story from Smith! He said something about special paper gowns with no metal particles—let me guess, you don't know where the gowns are!"

"Sorry," responded Jake as he and Val started violently stripping.

Jake could not help but notice her lovely body, bathed by the reddish-yellow lights of the flashing control panel. He quickly stuffed their clothing in a small bin underneath the control console, grabbed Val's hand, and pulled her into the magnet room. Jake ran to the side panel of the horizontal claw and pressed a red button about the size of a tennis ball, labeled ACTIVATE GANTRY. He simultaneously pulled Val down on the patient table located in the center of the now slowly closing claws.

"Jump on top of me," cried Jake. "We're about to enter the central magnetic field. Don't worry, as the claws close, the table will move in, giving us plenty of room within the magnet.

Ventilation will keep us comfortable. The guard won't be able to see us from his angle."

"Do I have an option?" asked Val in a rhetorical tone.

As the magnet claws closed, the three-tone chime of the outside door activated, followed by the hiss of an opening door. The patrol officer could have sworn that the claws were open the last time he was in the control room—then again, sometimes open, and sometimes closed. He saw it both ways often enough and that was not his business. He shined the flashlight into the magnet room nonetheless. It was protocol, and this was the military—leave independent thinking at the door!

Inside the bore of the magnet, Val's naked body lay on top of Jake's. Somehow Jake's concept of plenty of room was not the same as hers. Her breasts pressing hard against his chest, her mouth desperately trying to avoid the proximity of his lips. The rhythmic thump of the magnet drowned out all outside noise. They could barely see the circuitous path of the guard's flashlight through the hole in the magnetic bore, laying a careful pattern throughout the room. Any inside movement would be noticed even through the darkness.

"Jake," whispered Val. "Why is it that every time our paths cross, we end up naked and in the same position?"

"Animal magnetism," responded Jake with his unmistakable charming smile. "I read about it in *National Geographic*."

"I did, too," responded Val in a tone softer than before. "There was another article in the same issue—about the black widow spider and how she mates and then sucks the blood out of her mate. Be careful, my young and arrogant Han Solo!"

Perhaps it was the combination of the passionate kiss and the moment. The impending capture, their naked bodies touching as one. Their fear suddenly left and the proverbial ice had broken. Nothing was to come between them again.

Although awkward, Jake's first words after the kiss sealed their fate—sort of.

"Val, I never stopped loving you. I'm sorry—it was the wrong time in my career. Now let's get the fuck out of here—and by the way, I knew where the paper gowns were."

11

EXIT FROM EDEN

GETTING DRESSED TOOK almost as little time as getting undressed. Val grabbed the diskette from the backup CD burner. They exited the Tesla 6 room quietly, first looking down the corridor and then quietly but rapidly moving down the hallway. The initial video cameras were easily avoided. Jake knew every inch of Walter Reed.

Exit was far less complicated than entry, but then again, all things are relative. At least they had the CD diskette and presumably all of the evidence necessary to convince Kovalik or even the NSA that they were not crazy.

"What's the best way out?" asked Val.

"We need to get to the back of the hospital—the staff smoking area, that will lead us to the parking lot with no cameras on the way."

"You know, I don't look half bad on film," smirked Val. "I noticed that you managed to sneak a peek while I was undressing in the magnet."

"Jesus Christ, Val, I'm a doctor. Any attention I have ever given to the female form was purely professional," responded Jake. "Besides, don't get frisky on me now."

"Right!" muttered Val under her breath. "I don't think I have ever heard anyone use the words 'Jake,' 'women,' and 'professional' in the same sentence." Then again, here she was, more involved than ever.

They no longer needed to be careful with their security cards. The breach would be registered the moment Val used her card the first time, or within the routine 24-hour security sweep. Her card got them through the security doors like butter. Once in the main hospital wing, they were free—almost. They needed to get a pair of scrubs so that nobody would notice.

On entry to the nurse's on-call wing, Jake heard the characteristic rustling of keys of the patrol guard just around the corner. Val was startled by Jake's arm forcefully pushing her into the wall.

"Guard—" whispered Jake.

"Breast—" responded Val.

"What are you talking about?" asked Jake with a bewildered look.

"Your hand is on my breast. You can either keep it there until the guard comes, or we can dodge into an on-call room and hide."

Jake looked down, realizing that his right hand was plastered on Val's left breast as she hugged the wall. He pulled his hand away, grabbed hers, and pulled her into the adjacent on-call room.

As they gently closed the door to the room, they heard rustling in the bed adjacent to the window.

"Who's there?" whispered a woman's voice. A second later the click of a light went on.

Jake and Val turned in unison. Jake was about six foot two and Val was small and barely visible behind him.

"Oh, hi, Jake, I thought you were out of town. How did you know I was thinking about you last week?" asked a pretty young blonde nurse, obviously sleeping in the buff, sheets drawn up to half cover her breasts.

Val immediately jumped out from behind Jake and elbowed him in the ribs.

"Actually, blondie, Jake was on his honeymoon. We'll pick another room if you don't mind."

They opened the door slowly, peeked out, and left as rapidly as they entered.

"Well, easy come, easy go," sighed the blonde.

They grabbed a pair of scrub outfits in the empty call room next door and went out the back stairwell. They stopped momentarily in relief. Then a strong male voice behind them spoke. "Excuse me!" Jake and Val turned, shocked at the sight of a large security officer, gun holstered, standing right in front of them. His expression was, however, nonaggressive. They grabbed each other's hands and held tight. No matter what would happen next, doing nothing was the best thing they could do. Sort of like standing still in front of a growling German shepherd. If you run, you get bitten.

"You guys have a light? I have some smokes but no matches."

"Sorry," replied Val with a sheepish smile. "We really didn't come out here to smoke."

"Ah, to be young again," replied the guard as he turned and started walking back into the building.

Back at Val's apartment, they burst into the room and couldn't stop laughing. This was a master performance with the highest stakes. They now understood what a concert pianist must feel after a virtuoso performance.

Amidst the laughter, mixed with a little Merlot wine, their eyes met. Neither of them looked away. Jake's right hand gently grabbed Val's face and their lips softly touched. This time, Val's passion was unbridled. Val pushed Jake back on the couch and straddled his chest, still giggling.

"You know, Jake, you little shit, I knew where the paper gowns were, too. Smith showed me the locker while I was checking the T-6 breach."

She removed her black turtleneck and blue scrubs simultaneously. The dim light of the ever-present computer screens in Val's apartment silhouetted her body. Jake slowly lifted his body, sliding Val down on his hips. His mouth gently kissed her lips while his hands explored the lovely softness of her breasts. They had to make up for a lot of lost time and a lot of pain. Then again, as a famous comedian once said, "There is no better sex than makeup sex."

They spontaneously woke up in each other's arms at 1:20 am. Reality struck both of them like a sledgehammer. Val got up first and activated her UNIX computer. CD in place, she started sifting through the data. Jake stared at the sight of rapid computer keyboard typing and the fluorescent glare of a 21-inch monitor. He went to the kitchen and made some coffee.

"I have the medical data of six patient experiments," said Val, pointing to the screen. "I ran the patients through the FBI computer using my security clearance. All death row inmates. The interesting thing is that in each experiment, one patient is identified 'recipient.' Another patient is labeled 'donor.' I couldn't break the identity codes—until I noticed that each 'donor' was associated with a prison. When I cross-referenced the dates of the experiments with the prisons, guess what?"

"Execution—" muttered Jake.

"Yeah, how did you know?"

"That's how I would have done it," he responded, face down. "It's the perfect cover-up, Val. You fake the execution of the donor, take his life, and then bury him. Guess what—we just described the perfect crime. The person killed is already dead."

"Tell me, what of the 'recipients?'" asked Jake. "Any records?"

"Actually, Jake, that's what's interesting. All of the recipients were also on death row but had terminal diseases. Four had cancer, one terminal cirrhosis and liver failure, and the last had AIDS. They are all listed as 'dead of natural causes.' No evidence we can go after."

"Perfect," muttered Jake. "Let me see what medical tests were run."

Jake spent over an hour sifting through the extensive data. One thing can be said about the military—they're very methodical about recordkeeping.

"The results are all the same. The terminal cancer patients all had complete reversal of their disease processes. Look at this cancer patient. A five-centimeter lung mass is gone on the follow-up CT. Here is a terminal brain tumor patient with no mass left. Hopefully the EEGs will tell us something. No surgical procedure could have removed this tumor."

"There is something strange, though," murmured Jake. "I keep on getting back to that EEG article from England and the lifting sequence. Mrs. DeMarco acted funny after her cure. That has been haunting me for a long time. As Jones alluded, I am not sure these idiots understand exactly what is being transferred. The references are to the 'vital force' and rejuvenation. Maybe there is something more—Val, do you have a scanner?"

"Come on, Jake," responded Val with a smirk. "What kind of computer geek do you take me for? I have an industrial IBM drum scanner. It has the resolution to identify one of your pubic hairs from outer space!"

"Val, I can probably draw the line at scanning an old article I have for some EEG matches, although I may take you up on the pubic hair scan some other time," smiled Jake.

Jake proceeded to catalogue the pre- and post-experiment EEGs on Val's computer and index the scanned Hershberg lifting EEG trace pattern into the same database. He cross-referenced all of the appropriate links and then looked at the file size.

"Holy shit, Val, the tracings themselves are one terabyte of information. Cross-referencing Hershberg's lifting pulse multiplies the data by a factor of 12 with two sets of six patients per experiment. Twelve terabytes—that would take our Walter Reed computer about three years of processing time, and that's after I preprogrammed it to search out the right sequence."

"Three hours," mumbled Val.

"What's that?" asked Jake with a look of disbelief.

"I can get the Pentagon computer to run the data in three hours from my remote server right here. I'm already in deep shit. What's another breach with my name on it? I can always make up some bullshit line about a testing a new series of programming codes intended to fool the computer—in case we get out of this alive."

"In the meantime, I'll check out Mrs. DeMarco's address and pay her a visit. If I can get an EEG on a live patient and do some psychological testing, we may get some proof."

"Why are you hooked on this EEG crap?" asked Val. "Much of it sounds like supposition. The guy that wrote about the lifting got thrown out of medicine."

"I don't know, Val. You weren't there when the transfer occurred. It was something, Sergeant DeMarco dead on the floor and Mrs. DeMarco staring at the body with that strange look. I'm no shrink, but I've seen plenty of reaction to death. Val, what I saw was something different. When I talked to her afterward, it was as if she was someone else—I just can't explain it, Val."

"When you correlate it with the quantum singularity experiments that Einstein derived in a magnetic field, Abernathy Jones's strange response, and that EEG paper by Dr. Hershberg—it's just a feeling, Val, just a feeling."

"I tell you what," responded Val. "You go visit DeMarco, I'll get the EEG data completed from the Pentagon mainframe.

It will take me at least 12 hours to sort the data. We'll meet
tomorrow in Georgetown for a brew. I'll either prove you
right or wrong with this lifting thing. Let's meet at the Old
Stinger Pub at 1 pm. It's out of the way enough to give us
some cover."

12

DAY OF JUDGMENT

THE FAIRFAX COUNTY Penitentiary was just outside of Washington DC, approximately 30 minutes from the Pentagon. Project Lazarus was in full force. Once the verdict was passed, Morten Dublaise automatically entered the T-6 database as a "donor." All executed candidates were immediately placed in the T-6 database. There was, however, something special about his case. He was a rather atypical donor in that he had no noted illnesses and was in rather good shape for a man of his years.

Dr. Smith did not really care about the donor's mind. This was an experiment in the transfer of the vital force from one individual to another.

The other six experiments went superbly. Too bad the recipients had to be disposed of after the transfers. Even the government would not be able to explain to visiting family members with terminal cancers why their close ones all of a sudden looked cured and ten years younger. Their somewhat unexpected deaths were, however, very easy to explain. After all, they were terminal.

Dr. Smith was up for promotion to Lieutenant General and nothing was going to interfere with his breakthrough. The recipients were never allowed to wake up, but were placed into phenobarbital coma throughout the entire process. Once the transfer was completed, it usually took at least four weeks to run and repeat all of the tests—CT scans, repeat MRIs, EEGs, and complete blood profiles.

The locked ward at Walter Reed looked like a Frankenstein experiment. A row of comatose patients, artificially sustained for four to six weeks, monitored twenty-four hours a day. At the end of the "experiment" a lethal KCl injection put the "cured" patients into a fatal cardiac arrhythmia. Death was immediate.

After six patients, phase one of the experiment was over and Smith needed a new donor to enter phase two. This was to be the transfer of the life force into a healthy volunteer. This was the step the Pentagon was waiting for.

His last pentagon report was a clear success. It was personally presented to the Joint Committee. He has never seen the brass so attentive. Kovalik sat in the front row, beaming with his newfound pride. Finally, the credit the NIH and Walter Reed deserved. Kovalik knew that Smith could pull this off. Plagiarism is the sincerest form of flattery, and Smith was a world-class flatterer.

The transfer of the vital force into a Navy Seal volunteer could be the start of what Smith dubbed the new breed of fighting machine. All indicators pointed to enhanced T-cell immune activity and enhanced ribosomal healing activity, and there was nothing to keep Smith from extrapolating and wowing his enthusiastic audience with the potential of enhanced strength and vision, even enhanced IQ. The preliminary muscle stimulation activity pointed to contractile strength three times that of normal muscle tissue. The birth of the ultimate fighting machine.

To Navy Seals the term *volunteers* was an oxymoron. The Seals were by definition volunteers. They were operatives, snipers, and assassins. They did what was necessary. The more covert the assignment, the more volunteers there were.

Smith got immediate permission to proceed. The operation was BlackIce, and five volunteer Navy Seals were immediately selected. Unfortunately, according to Smith, the Democrats had made our country soft and executions were few and far between. This next donor would have to be special. He needed to have a clean medical history. Like the Nazis who had tried but failed, Smith was about to create the "Übermensch"—the super being! Dublaise was the ideal medical donor. Fate worked again!

The execution harvesting was the easy part. A faked execution followed by induction of a phenobarbital coma. The bodies could last in this state for weeks. Unfortunately, he had no bodies—until Dublaise.

The gallows chamber in sub-basement 3 of the Manassas State Penitentiary was as expected. A stark room with tile walls, an upright chair containing head, arm, and leg straps, and an IV setup on a pole immediately to the left of the patient. The lethal injection was a custom three-drug combination consisting of a sedative, a deep narcotic, and a cardiac arrythmogenic. It was simply called the "cocktail" by the inmates.

Immediately in front of the gallows was a one-way reflective mirror. Today the gallery was full. The relatives of Dublaise' victims were allowed to watch the execution. It was to be the end of their personal ordeal.

Outside the prison walls, hundreds of Dublaise faction members were petitioning. The signs were everywhere:

"You are killing the Messiah"

"Revenge will be ours"

"Armageddon."

Within the chamber walls, the well-rehearsed performance was set. The Virginia state executioner became mysteriously ill and could not attend this landmark execution. The substitute executioner was accompanied by an unusually large contingent, to protect him from potential harm. As required by law, the lethal injection was mixed in front of four witnesses—hand-selected, of course. Two vials of phenobarbital, carefully titrated for body weight, replaced the sedative and arrythmogenic. The first vial was diprovan, a deep and severe respiratory depressant.

The induction of coma and shallow respiration mimicking death was scientifically planned with the precision of a staged magic act. A funeral van was waiting. It was a large black van labeled "Medical Examiner." On the inside, a full ambulance and operating room, equipped for full resuscitation and body preservation.

Diprovan was the key drug, effective but dangerous. Only certified anesthesiologists are allowed to use it because of its incredibly tight safety margin. They call it a "tight LD-50," medical jargon for the dose that will kill 50 percent of all recipients. For most drugs, the margin of error is 30 to 40 percent. For Diprovan, it is less than 10 percent, with variable results in each patient. That is why two inmates died in the early experiments. Smith learned the hard way that he needed an anesthesiologist on board—but then again, who cares about a bunch of death row inmates?

Dublaise refused a blindfold. He entered the chamber, looked at the one-way mirror, and smiled, his right forefinger rubbing the inside of his collar.

"Salvation shall be mine, my friends. Your children and loved ones were the first to be harvested, and shall be the first to see my glory!"

His speech was truncated by a rough prison guard as Dublaise was pushed into the gallows chair and strapped. A priest then presented a Bible for the prisoner to hold. Dublaise laughed and threw it on the floor.

The injection took seconds to react. A rigged EKG monitor was electronically synchronized to beep a flat-line EKG as the apparently lifeless body of Dublaise went limp. The resuscitation team inside the converted funeral van was ready for intubation and coma induction. The body was immediately packed in dry ice and hypothermia was induced to prevent any potential brain damage.

At about the same time, Jake met Manny Rodriguez at Bud's for the last time. They did not talk but sat next to each other, watching the local coeds rhythmically gyrate their hips while disrobing in front of several dozen horny servicemen. What the hell, the tips were good and there was a no-touch policy that even the President of the United States would have to abide by.

Manny nonchalantly turned to Jake and said, "Hey, buddy, got change for a five? Need those singles to stick in their garter belts, otherwise they won't come close."

"Yeah, I know what you mean," Jake responded, counting out five singles.

Manny handed Jake a five-dollar bill, neatly folded. On the inside, a piece of paper with an address:

Ginny DeMarco 2342 Potomac Drive Gaithersburg, MD

Jake knocked on the front door of a middle-class neighborhood. The cab ride had taken about 45 minutes in noon traffic. A pretty young lady answered the door.

"Can I help you?"

"Yes, ma'am, I'm Lieutenant Jake Eriksson from Walter Reed. I'm just following up on how your mother is doing," responded Jake, not knowing how he would answer any questions about being out of uniform.

"Can't you guys just leave my mother alone? She's unchanged since your last visit. It's as if she's lost her mind. She's not sick, but she's not the same. She just sits outside on the patio, smoking cigars. That's the weirdest thing," she continued. "She hated Dad's cigars, but I figure maybe it's some kind of transference and mourning thing."

"I know this may be very hard for you, but would it be possible to run brain wave tests? They're called EEGs. They don't hurt at all but it may help us figure what is going on. I can even bring the machine here so that it won't inconvenience you or your mother."

Jake figured there was probably no way he could get consent to bring Mrs. DeMarco into Walter Reed, but he knew where they kept the backup EEG unit in the basement storage area. The boys in storage owed him a couple of favors and he knew nobody would miss the unit for a few hours. The machine was the size of a microwave and had its own wheels. Bringing it to the house would be no problem.

Skinny Mrs. DeMarco on the patio, legs crossed, smoking a large Churchill cigar in a pink robe with a fuzzy collar, was quite a sight. She hadn't shaved her legs for at least two months. A half-empty bottle of Bud was on the table next to her.

"Mrs. DeMarco, may I have a moment with you?" asked Jake.

Mrs. DeMarco looked up with a glazed stare of disbelief. The primal anger emanating from the eyes of this rather demure woman was paralyzing to Jake. He was frozen, like a deer staring into the lights of an oncoming truck. Her outburst was rapid and Jake had no time to react.

"You fucking son of a bitch! You've gotta lot of nerve showing up here. What did you do with Ginny? What the fuck did you do with her? I'm a damn monster— "

Her right cross-landed squarely on Jake's jaw. The amount of power generated by this elderly woman surprised him. The next two punches, however, were even more surprising. A left upper cut to the stomach followed by a straight right jab at Jake's left eye. The punches hit firmly and rhythmically. Had there been more mass behind them, Jake would have probably been knocked unconscious, but he just lay on the grass, bleeding from his lip and holding his eye. His confusion was only matched by his inability to gasp for air. The stomach punch had knocked the wind out of his lungs.

Just as Mrs. DeMarco was about to come in for another round, a large male figure grabbed her and lifted her in the air, kicking and screaming profanity. "I don't know what you want, but you better get the hell out of here," he shouted. Jake noticed Mrs. DeMarco's daughter in the corner of his good eye, hands on her mouth, crying. Jake immediately realized the large man was her husband, protecting the household.

On leaving the house, Jake remembered his first meeting with Sergeant DeMarco as if it were yesterday. "I was all-division boxing champion in 1972 . . . " he had said.

13

AN AFTERNOON TO REMEMBER

AFFAIRS OF STATE were often a bore to President Sumner. This afternoon's dedication was no different He knew everyone was expecting some statement about the presidential stay of execution Reverend Dublaise—the call that never came. The president was staunchly against capital punishment. The execution, however, occurred as planned.

Then came the expected picket lines outside the Smithsonian after the execution—and the heightened security. The only thing he would enjoy was seeing his old friend Peter Kovalik. This was the end of Sumner's first term in office. His repeated attempts to get Peter more involved with politics were a dismal failure.

"David, you know me better than that," Kovalik would answer. "I'm just a dumb Polack running Walter Reed. I let you smartass West Point graduates fuck up the country and you don't need my help—you all do just fine!"

The demonstrations outside were somewhat more rowdy than expected. Picket signs calling Sumner "the Judas of Washington" were everywhere. Security was tight.

Inside the Smithsonian, the dedication of the new Ming Dynasty wing went on as planned. The last thing the Sumner administration wanted to do was pay undue attention to the Dublaise faction. They were to be treated as a nuisance at most.

China's most-favored-nation status was of course the root of the event, but in the background the new Chinese government donated a wing of priceless relics in the name of détente. Sumner called it "in the name of bullshit" behind closed doors, but his gracious acceptance speech was nonetheless expected and executed with his usual presidential charm.

"Ah, President Sumner!" shouted Senator Brooks from Texas. "May I have a word?"

Sumner despised Brooks, He was a Bible-beating right-wing conservative, an outspoken supporter of paramilitary groups and probably the next right-wing candidate for the presidency. Sumner turned rapidly towards his wife to try to head in the opposite direction, but was unable to execute the maneuver before Brooks cut them off.

"You know, Mr. President, Dublaise had a lot of sympathizers in Texas. They expected a life sentence for him—following your pardon. A lot of people in this country believe in the right to defend themselves, unlike your cabinet."

Sumner could not respond the way he wanted to but was boiling inside. The President did not have the liberties of emotion afforded most common folk. He was often reminded of that by his wife.

Brooks was obnoxious enough when sober. After a few martinis—"I know the President also believes in defending personal rights and this very nation, sir," exclaimed a clearly irritated voice immediately behind Brooks. It was Kovalik, smiling from ear to ear.

"Who may you be?" retorted Brooks with due annoyance. "I believe I was talking to the President, not you."

David Sumner's wife responded immediately. "This is Dr. Paul Kovalik, Senator Brooks. He and David served in Vietnam. Paul is head of Walter Reed and may become the next Surgeon General," smiled Nancy, knowing she was killing two birds with one stone. Paul and Nancy Sumner had done this before. David had a short fuse with idiots. Sometimes saying what was on his mind was a political mistake, especially in an election year.

"I heard about you," retorted Brooks while turning back to the president. "This is the guy whose ass you saved on that hill in Nam—got you the Purple Heart and Silver Star."

Sumner immediately turned and walked away.

"What's got a bug up his ass?" asked Brooks.

"Senator Brooks," replied Nancy Sumner with the composure of a First Lady. "David is a very open person, but in my 30 years of knowing him, there is only one off-limit subject, and that is his Vietnam medals. He discusses them with nobody, not even Dr. Kovalik. It is simply taboo, and we all respect his wishes. You see, he has always felt that Peter deserved the medals and did not want anybody to think he got them because he was a Senator's son. You see, sir, my husband is a man of integrity!"

With that comment, both Peter Kovalik and Nancy Sumner joined the President.

On approach, Nancy gently put her right arm inside the fold of the President's elbow, giving him a gentle "I understand" hug.

"Thanks, dear," whispered the President. He then turned to Peter. "Would you like to join us in the White House for an afternoon movie and quiet dinner, Peter? I used my influence to get the prerelease director's cut of *The Matrix V* and I know how much you like that mind transfer sci-fi stuff. I think I've about had it with this dedication."

"As long as you get me a cab after the movie, David," smiled Peter Kovalik. "You know how hard it is to get a late cab in DC." They truly were the best of friends.

The presidential exit towards the door was a well-orchestrated Secret Service operation. Sumner gave a clandestine sign to the alpha agent and the slow progress towards the door started. The 12 Secret Service agents scattered throughout the building assumed exit posts. Microphone communications alerted the 30 outdoor agents, all dressed in civilian clothes with wireless earplugs imperceptible to even the most experienced operative.

The noise and petition signs outside the majestic main entrance to the Smithsonian gallery were near deafening. This was a Secret Service nightmare. The agents, dressed in black, started parting the crowd in preparation for the President. The limo was in position at the bottom of the stairwell. A black Ford Expedition was immediately behind and two black Lincoln Continentals were in front of the presidential limo.

A pretty twenty-year-old woman was slowly strolling her baby across the grassy area on the quadrangle opposite the museum. Seeing the increasing activity, she turned and started heading towards the museum. She had never seen the President up close and this was her opportunity. There was excitement in the air. Her baby was a pretty little blonde thing, about 18 months old and quite well-behaved, fascinated by the crowd and noise.

They approached the south side of the Smithsonian, most people letting a woman with a baby carriage right through. The occasional denser crowd was immediately parted by the young woman's gentle but direct voice: "Excuse me, I'm trying to get to my husband!" She finally had the perfect view. There was excitement in her eyes.

The president was flanked by Nancy on his right and a proud Dr. Paul Kovalik on his left. Standard Secret Service cover just to the outside of the entourage, behind, and in front. Senator Brooks, always an opportunist, elbowed himself right behind the President—nothing like a little free press with the leader of the free world.

The side view the young woman had was great. It was a straight line of sight of the President between the front Secret Service officer and the left flanking officer. The President was coming down at a good pace, approximately 25 yards away. The baby started crying, as if something had suddenly pinched it. "Oh, my sweetie, you must be hungry," exclaimed the young woman as reaching down to get a bottle from the kangaroo pouch behind the carriage.

The following events were blinding fast. She removed a stainless steel .357 Magnum snub nose pistol and fired three rounds of Glaser slugs in approximately two seconds. Glasers have been outlawed by most states because they act like shrapnel when they hit someone. Even an off-target hit can kill. The fourth round was interrupted by a flying tackle from a nearby agent shouting "Gun!" The round did go off, but it was muffled.

The baby was crying hysterically. The young woman was on her back underneath a 220-pound Secret Service agent, blood everywhere. There was panic and mayhem.

The President was immediately grabbed and shrouded by Kovalik on the left and the right flanking Secret Service officer. Blood was all over the presidential party. Nancy Sumner's face was covered with blood and hair containing skull fragments. The left flanking officer was shouting "Man down! Man down!" and all handguns and submachine guns were drawn. "Get the President out of here—is he hurt?" It was impossible to tell who was injured with all the blood around. Senator Brooks's body was, however, motionless, lying on the steps. A direct head wound had shattered his skull, as if it were a scene from the Kennedy assassination. The presidential party was immediately rushed to the safety of the limo. Rule number one—get the President out of the hot zone and then assess the injuries!

In the presidential limo, Kovalik immediately started examining the President. His pulse was tachycardic and there was no apparent bleeding site and no evidence of a penetrating wound. Nancy was shaking hysterically. The accompanying officer, James Matthews, was strong, gentle, and intensely dedicated to the first family. He would do anything for them. He watched intently while hugging Nancy. One word from him and the limo would be immediately diverted to the nearest prescribed hospital. Matthews was the charge officer. He whispered into his collar microphone, "Angel one, clear so far, proceed to White House."

"Jesus, Paul, that reminded me of Nam," said Sumner, out of breath, patting himself down to make sure he was OK. "Dodged another one. I hope they don't write another shit story about this."

"Yeah, David. Seems like you have as many lives as a cat," smiled Kovalik.

As he gently grasped Sumner's shoulder, he noticed a subtle facial droop. Sumner started becoming agitated.

"Paul, there's something www...rr...on...nng—"

David Sumner started seizing uncontrollably. His facial droop accentuated and the seizures were only involving the right side of his body. Officer Matthews stared. Kovalik took over.

"Divert to Walter Reed STAT. Call ahead, delta code PRESIDENT BLUE. Clear Trauma Bay One for intubation and get anesthesia down NOW! Clear CT for emergency brain scan."

The limo burst into the Walter Reed Emergency Bay and all staff was at the ready. This is the nightmare drill scenario that the staff rehearsed with the secret service at least twenty times per year. Called "Capital Blue," it was set up for any high-ranking government official. The drill involved medicine, surgery, internal security, and the Secret Service. It was the only time loaded guns were allowed in the trauma bay—a federal regulation.

The President was STAT intubated and phenobarbital stabilized the seizures by placing him in an immediate coma. The CT results were shown to Kovalik, the Chief of Neurology, and the Chief of Neurosurgery as soon as the films were pulled out of the processor. The look on their faces told the whole tale. The news was very bad. The President had suffered a major stroke, induced by the day's events and a history of chronic hypertension. The newspapers and TV cameras were already swarming Walter Reed.

The critical staff entered executive session so that they could deal first and foremost with the President, but then with the press. They clearly needed to control all information leaking out of the hospital. The news would affect world politics.

14

THE AWAKENING

THE SIGHT of Jake entering the Old Stinger Pub in Georgetown was comical at best. One hand was over his bruised eye and the other rubbing his sore chin. The bouncer guarding the door barely let him in. "Can I help you, sir?"

"No," responded Jake with a scowl. He was in no mood for pleasantries.

"Now listen, buddy, we run a clean establishment, but if you want trouble, you came to the right place."

At this point the bouncer felt a gentle tap on his shoulder. It was obvious that the volume of the conversation was a bit higher than anyone wanted. The bouncer assumed it was the boss.

When he turned around, Jake was surprised to see Val with a big, bright smile on her face.

"Sorry, sir, this is my misfit brother—always getting into a fight because he can't keep his nose out of trouble," smiled Val. "I'll take him of your hands and you won't have any more trouble—sugar!"

Val had this incredible way of acting the bimbo and soothing the hearts of even the most savage beast. She turned it on at will. This time, she knew that if she had not interceded, Jake's face would look worse on the way out than on the way in.

"Jake, you look like you hit a truck. I thought all you were going to do was get permission to do an EEG on Mrs. DeMarco. Looks like you tried to beat the shit out of her and failed," smiled Val. Somehow, Jake found no humor in her flippant comments.

"Val, you don't know how close to the truth you are. She did beat the shit out of me, but it wasn't Ginny DeMarco. Remember I told you that Sergeant DeMarco was a boxing champion in the Marines—he won the title one year?"

"Yeah, so what does that have to do with it—did he come back from the grave to protect his wife?" asked Val.

"Well, do you remember that I told you there was something strange about Mrs. DeMarco after the scan and the death of her husband? I think I figured out what," he said, rubbing his jaw. "I found her smoking a big cigar. She spoke to me in a very disoriented manner, but all of a sudden two things connected. Her fist and my jaw. While bleeding on the lawn, I realized that what she was saying all along made perfect sense—only if she was Sergeant DeMarco."

"Well, Jake, you're not going to believe this, but the Pentagon mainframe may support what you are saying."

Val took out a manila folder with about 200 pages of printed computer data.

"Look at the cross-matched sequences. I did just what you asked me to do. We have the donor EEG and the recipient EEG right here, and a cross-match of the Hershberg lifting trace for all sequences. They are there, on every one. Not only that, but the EEG sequences of the donor became imprinted in the recipient. Look—the lifting sequence is here in every case."

Jake's eyes were wide open. Unlike Val, he was capable of reading EEG squiggles as if reading a novel. He started turning the pages of data furiously. Patient by patient, Jake's expression turned from despair to elation. "Val, you're brilliant. There is no way Kovalik could have possibly cross-matched these sequences, and I'm sure Smith and those monkeys working with him can't distinguish the EEGs of dogs from humans. We have it!"

First the pulse sequence inducing the lifting EEG finger-print, then the transition of the donor's characteristic frontal lobe EEG to the recipient.

"Jake, I understand the lifting pulse, but what does the frontal lobe EEG have to do with anything?"

"Personality, Val—personality! You see, the frontal lobe defines us as individuals—remember Jack Nicholson in *Cuckoo's Nest*? When they gave him a lobotomy he lost his personality. What we are seeing here is a transfer—not only the vital force, but also the 'soul.' I'm not religious, but if I were God, I would put the soul in the frontal lobes and in the hippocampus. The rest of the brain just does the grunt work."

Val just stared into space.

"So the soul survives. Talk about Frankenstein! We have to tell them, Jake. This can result in disaster. We have to tell Kovalik—or even the newspapers," insisted Val as her voice became more agitated.

Their quiet conversation was broken by intense commotion at the bar. At least fifteen people gathered round the TV set. The bartender was increasing the volume—it looked like they were watching a press conference.

Jake and Val slowly gathered their stuff and made their way to the bar. The news anchor was blazing—

"—As we are all waiting anxiously for news regarding the presidential assassination attempt and possible life-threatening injuries to President Sumner, perhaps this nation's most beloved president since JFK." The newscaster began fumbling with his lapel mike and earplug.

"I have an announcement from the Chief of Staff—we are cutting to the inside of Walter Reed, where Dr. Paul Kovalik, the President's personal physician, will update the nation."

"Kovalik," whispered Jake and Val nearly simultaneously.

A distinguished Kovalik almost immediately appeared on the TV screen, X-ray light box immediately behind him containing images from the CT scan of the President's brain.

"Ladies and gentlemen of the press. Approximately two hours ago, a failed assassination attempt was made on the President of the United States. Although uninjured by any bullets, the President suffered a stroke in this area of the brain." Kovalik pointed at the CT scan.

Jake pushed two customers aside and jumped on the bar counter to get a better look at the CT scans. It was a comical scene. The bartender had never quite seen a customer climb onto the bar before, not even on Super Bowl Sunday.

"Hey, asshole, you want to get down so the rest of us can see!" shouted one of the customers. Jake's favorite bouncer immediately took notice, but even Val could not save him this time.

"I've had it with you college assholes—no respect for other people. This is it for you, now get the fuck out of here before I work your face over more than the last guy that went at you!"

With those words, Val and Jake were tossed out of the bar.

"Gee, you just never lose your touch, do you, Jake?"

"Oh, I've got thrown out of better places. Besides, I was looking at the CT and I needed a closer view. The President is fucked! I don't care what spin Kovalik puts on it, what I saw was a major hemorrhagic infarction."

"Well, I'm sorry to hear that. Sumner is really a good president."

"Was—" responded Jake. "The guy's brain is a vege-matic."

"Sensitive, Jake. Real sensitive. Now I know why you really went into neuroradiology. It's your wonderful bedside manner. Anyway, we're still in big shit, and despite this tragedy, we have to go back to my place. I have some ideas."

15

NIGHT MOVES

THE RIDE HOME was quiet. Both Val and Jake were thinking intently. Once back at the apartment, Val immediately logged onto the computer and started typing code that was truly foreign to Jake. The only thing he noticed was that she was on the secure State Department server and was furiously copying files from one computer to the other.

"What, no pleasantries or small talk, Val?" asked Jake with a smile.

"You know, you look like an idiot with that black eye—the only funnier thought is that you got it from a little old lady."

"Well, I guess I asked for that, but what the hell are you doing?" asked Jake.

"You know those porno Spam notes everyone gets that ever logged onto a site? Well, I'm making a similar e-mail bomb that acts like a virus. If we don't turn it off in 48 hours, all of the information I put in here first goes to the Senate Judiciary Committee and the Pentagon/NSC and then in 24 more hours to the *New York Times* and *Wall Street Journal*. The State Department return e-mail address and my BlackIce security code will guarantee attention. They won't be able to block the mailing—can't break my security codes. It's coming from me, Jake—I'm really running the gauntlet with you now."

"Now you're scaring me, Val. What are *we* including in this virus bomb thing?"

"You can help with the medical lingo. I figure we outline a complete explanation of your project, the data from the secure T-6 server, and the EEGs with your Pentagon computer lifting sequence interpretation and frontal lobe transition from donor to recipient. That should raise some eyebrows.

"Not only that, but I identified the tampering with your file and wrote code that will reverse all hacker changes by downloading and reinserting the backup file copy. The jerk who messed with your file does not know that my code has something I call on-the-fly mirroring. I wrote the defense program, which basically double copies all files to a remote part of the server simultaneously as the information is written. That way, if someone tampers with the info, I have a hidden 'pure copy' right on a partition of the same hard drive.

"Anyway, it's clear even to a nonmedical person like me. The government took over your project but didn't understand what they were messing with."

"What if something happens and we want to stop the letter?"

"Jake, just log on and type in the word 'Tantalus.' You remember, the Greek half-god who was the favored son of Zeus, until he shared the forbidden food of the gods. Zeus cursed him by eternally tantalizing him with all human needs and desires, only to take them away at the very last minute," smiled Val.

"You're right, Val. They think they're transferring only the vital force and life from one person to the other, when they're transferring the entire being—the soul! But we can't just send this—we need to talk to Kovalik. Give him one more chance."

"He's military, but he's not a fool. I need to get Mrs. DeMarco to Walter Reed. Nothing will convince him more than a live patient with an EEG and psychological profile."

As Jake finished his sentence, Val started dialing the number she saw on the yellow pad next to the telephone.

"Hello, this is Nurse Smith at the Walter Reed Army Medical Center department of neurology. We have a scheduled appointment for a Mrs. DeMarco tomorrow at 8 am. Are you her daughter?"

Val's southern accent was accompanied by a wink at Jake. She was smooth—get Mrs. DeMarco in the building tomorrow and they could figure out the rest! Jake could not help but smile. But suddenly Val's face changed. She was listening to the person on the other side intently.

"I'm so sorry, we didn't know," whispered Val into the phone, covering her eyes. Tears started rolling down her cheeks. For the first time, Val was crying and outwardly despondent.

"What?" asked Jake. "What's going on?"

"They found her right after you left, Jake. She just took a rope, threw it over a tree branch, tied it around her neck, and then jumped off a chair. She killed herself, Jake—she killed herself because she couldn't take what she had become. What have you created, Jake? What have you created with your brilliance?"

Back at Walter Reed, the T-6 scanner was being activated and the usual security team was in position, including lovely Susan Carlson at the console and a somewhat demure man dressed in an old tweed suit helping with the controls. As the machine was warming up, an ambulance crew was strapping the body of Reverend Dublaise on to the gurney immediately outside the main bore. In the anteroom, a prisoner in shackles was being prepared for transfer by another team of technologists and nurses.

"Susan, I want to thank you for kindly explaining everything you are doing. I feel as if I could run the machine myself," remarked Abernathy Jones.

"Dr. Jones, it is my pleasure to have someone as distinguished as yourself on this project. It's not often that Dr.

Kovalik and Dr. Smith are overruled on a decision," smiled Susan. "You know, they think you are some kind of Pentagon spy, but I think you're just an adorable guy—besides, a trained monkey can run this scanner. All of the transfer programming is now built into the computer and standardized."

Abernathy had to resist saying what he was thinking. In all actuality, a trained monkey was at the controls. She just happened to be a trained monkey with a tight blouse and incredible body.

While Susan entered the patient's name and demographics, Abernathy manned the control console and activated the critical pulse sequences as if he had been doing this all of his life. Susan was entirely correct, but Abernathy was not a "trained monkey" but a Nobel Prize laureate.

The door to the T-6 room opened somewhat more briskly than usual and Kovalik appeared with a scowl on his face. Abernathy glanced over as Kovalik whispered something in Susan's ear and then went over to the chief of security. Within seconds, all but Susan Carlson left the room. After finishing the console programming, she promptly got up and left.

"Dr. Jones," remarked Kovalik with an unmistakable authoritative voice. "Our plans have changed. We are not running the sequence on the prisoner we originally intended and I'm afraid you will have to leave the project room. This is now a Level 1 BlackIce Operation authorized by the NSA and Secret Service. No unauthorized personnel."

"Dr. Kovalik, you don't seem to understand. I am the NSA. I am cleared for BlackIce operations you cannot even conceive of. Don't force me to pull strings. I have been following the day's events. If this is what I think it is, you probably want as few people here as possible, but you need the right people.

"Besides, I saw the twinkie walk out of the room. You need me to help run the scanner. When is the last time you ran the protocol? If something goes wrong, you're screwed. I have memorized all of the specs and ran the last two transfer patients."

Kovalik had no choice. A decision had to be made and the President's life was on the line. He picked up the phone, punched the extension, and said, "Activate Lazarus Prime on my directive, Now!"

This was the order—"Lazarus Prime." The culmination of unproven technology, nonscientific methodology, and alchemy in an experiment on the dying leader of the free world.

"I must be fuckin' crazy," mumbled Kovalik.

16

BLUES IN THE MORNING

JAKE AND VAL slept very little that night. They were passionate, but even their rekindled love somehow seemed inappropriate given the moment. The sex was good, but it was reminiscent of a condemned person's last meal—tasty but probably never to be enjoyed again. Their concern was reflected in a lover's embrace, which brought them the few hours of sleep they so desperately needed.

They both spontaneously awoke at 6 am and started planning the next move. Val immediately went to her computer. Jake noticed this as a recurring theme. He wondered if she was one of those few people capable of thinking cognitively in their sleep, only to awaken with new and novel ideas not present prior to sleep.

She accessed the security mainframe and started typing. Jake just watched with amazement as cryptic code rushed across the screen. He identified several foreign languages as Val bounced off remote servers. First Italian, then either Bulgarian or Hungarian, and finally some Arabic symbols. It suddenly dawned on him that Val spoke all of those languages fluently. She was as deep in the spook business as one can get.

"What are you hacking into now?" asked Jake.

"Trying to buy us more time," responded Val. "I am forcing a real intrusion into the NSA mainframe. The goal is to get caught this time. The finger, of course, will be pointing to some Islamic separatist group. I figure by using a Middle

Eastern hacking technique, my division will be busting ass for
at least three days. I am about four layers deep into our security
computers, just short of our nuclear defense dispersion plans.
Then I will purposely fall into my own hacker intrusion trap.
When that happens, bells will go off from the NSA to the
Pentagon signaling a major breach. They won't know how
much information has been compromised until they run a
full diagnostic. Kind of like the Microsoft intrusion in October
2000."

"That was the trick-or-treat Halloween of the century. It
took my division three months to track down the hacker and
analyze just how much of the Windows source code she got.
Damn, the hacker was good—reminded me of my younger
days!"

"How will that help us?"

"Well, Jake, once they get the alarm, they won't run the
conventional low-level security scans because they won't have
the staff or time. They won't detect my illegal pass use. That
gives us a few days since the Walter Reed security scans have
low priority. If we ever get out of this alive, they will have to
call me to track down the intrusion since I wrote the hunter
killer code. Anything deeper than a Level 2 breach needs my
analysis by protocol—since I wrote the protocol."

"Once in, I can cover our tracks at Walter Reed before
they track our entry using the standard sweep. Walter Reed
and NIH are such low security risks that we can probably get
away with our breach at T-6, that is, if we are out of prison."
Somehow Val's voice was not as confident as in the past.

Back at Walter Reed, the T-6 lab was uncharacteristically
staffed. Kovalik was watching the vital signs and monitoring
the pulse sequence programmed by Abernathy Jones. The
President's chief Secret Service officer attentively watching
the magnet. It was a strange sight, the President in the magnet
and Reverend Morten Dublaise strapped outside the magnet,

one hand tied to President Sumner's left foot, forcing physical contact. Officer Matthews was trained to observe everything. This was his second presidential term assignment and he understood the rules. Never question unless the President was in harm's way. In this case, it was obvious that the President was critical and something very unusual was going on. It was also very obvious that the President's life was at stake. His job was to give his life for the President, not to question.

Kovalik noticed the officer staring at the gold mesh wall. He knew the code of the Secret Service, but he also knew men. Especially military types. They responded to respect, structure, and a strict code. Kovalik slowly walked over, knowing that he had two hours to kill and the future of the presidency to protect.

"I'm sorry, officer. In the rush to save the President, I did not introduce myself. I am General Paul Kovalik."

"Officer James Matthews, sir."

"Well, James, may I call you that?" asked Kovalik in a tone that left no question as to who was in command. He started talking before Matthews could even utter words of agreement.

"Do you have any questions about what is going on here, James?"

"No, sir," responded Matthews with a near-robotic response.

Kovalik recognized covert operations training a mile away. Matthews had a deep military background. Perhaps Seal or Special CIA Ops. It was fairly common to have the President's number one man a trained killer. The job demanded discipline beyond the scope of most training programs.

"Nonetheless, I want to explain to you that what you are seeing never happened. This project does not exist. If we manage to save the life of the President, it is by the transfer of the life force of a known killer. If this gets out, the implications to the President and national security are dire."

"General Kovalik," responded Matthews with a tone that resounded conviction. "I have BlackIce clearance and have worked on many sensitive covert assignments. I answer only to the President and will sacrifice my life if necessary. I now pledge my allegiance not only to the President but also to you. President Sumner has been kind to me. You spend a lot of time in close quarters with the President in a position such as mine. He's a good man. I can tell that you are too."

"I'm glad, James. I may have to ask you to do some things in the future. Things that may seem unusual. Do you understand, James?" asked Kovalik while looking over his shoulders at Jones at the console.

"I understand," responded Matthews with an icy tone. There was no question in Kovalik's mind. Matthews was a loaded gun. Men like Matthews were like switches. Once activated, they responded without thought.

"Twenty minutes to go," said Abernathy Jones in the background.

Back at the apartment, Val was finishing up on the computer and Jake had started cooking breakfast. Ham and cheese omelets were his specialty. It was bound to be a long day and breakfast might be their only meal. Val never wanted to break Jake's heart by telling him that the purpose of garlic in omelets was to add a little flavor, not to protect them from a vampire attack.

As he clicked the electric coffee pot on, he picked up the remote and turned the kitchen TV on. The news about the President was bound to be grave—a complicating factor. Jake's plans were to attempt to contact Kovalik one final time and to convince him about the "soul transfer"—this time with hard evidence and an e-mail bomb threat. He just wished he had Mrs. DeMarco as a live witness—too bad!

Val looked tired and her hair was uncombed, but Jake stared at her beauty. She was not the most gentle or feminine of women. She exuded self-confidence and a near-arrogance in everything she did. Then, as if by magic, she could convert to a soft feminine temptress. They were quite a match for each other.

"Another day in paradise, Jake," smiled Val with her best snide face. She slowly poured a cup of black coffee and turned to the TV under her kitchen counter.

"Would you put on CNN?" asked Jake. "I want to hear what happened to the President. If he died last night, I doubt Kovalik will be receptive to anything we have to say. Our job will be just that much harder."

"Val, we really need that asshole as an ally."

"—In one of the most miraculous medical interventions, neuroradiologists reversed the President's stroke last night. Here explaining the procedure is Dr. Paul Kovalik, Chief of Staff at Walter Reed Medical Center and the President's personal physician."

Paul Kovalik looked as if he had not slept all night. He was concise in his statements. Both Val and Jake stared at the TV in disbelief.

"Ladies and gentlemen of the press. Yesterday I faced you and our nation with the gravest of news. Today I am fortunate to report that our medical team worked through the night and infused a clot-busting drug called TPA directly into the President's brain. This drug has been used for years in the heart and has just recently been used directly in the brain. With heroic measures, we managed to melt all of the clot and completely reverse the stroke. The President awoke briefly this morning, moving all four extremities. He also mumbled several words."

The newsroom exploded with activity, hands raised with questions.

"Dr. Kovalik!" shouted a young male reporter in the front row. "What were the President's first words?"

" 'Where the hell am I?' " smiled Kovalik.

Jake stared at the TV and started shouting uncontrollably.

"Bullshit! Bullshit! They fuckin' did it, Val. I can't believe this!"

"What are you talking about, Jake? This sounds great—the President was saved by Kovalik. They saved him!"

"Val, that's impossible. Do you remember me climbing on the bar to look at the CAT scan on the TV?"

"Yeah, Jake. That was the smooth move that got you thrown out on your ear!"

"Never mind that, Val. What I saw in the President's brain scan was blood. You see, Val, blood looks white on the CT scanner when it's fresh. That's called a 'hemorrhagic infarction.' The president was bleeding into his brain. That is an absolute contraindication to the clot buster TPA."

"You see, all TPA would do is cause more bleeding. Death would be instantaneous. We proved that at Mass General during my Neuroradiology Fellowship. Three patients died before the FDA warning went out. Even the slightest amount of blood is a contraindication. I can show you the contraindications on the drug formulary in print."

Val looked confused. It still didn't make any sense. "Jake, what are you saying?"

"They ran the experiment—on the President. Those fuckin' idiots. They don't understand. The soul survives! The soul survives! They didn't revive the president. They just put someone else into his body, consciousness and all."

Val had no time for sentiment or self-pity. She understood that they were in deep trouble. This new disaster was bound to mean even more trouble for them. The question was, how much?

She headed for the Unix mainframe computer and logged on. Jake looked up and was surprised at her focused actions. She was searching for something.

"Val, what are you after?"

"If you're right, Jake, then not only do they not know what they are doing, but they needed a recent donor. I am searching the FBI database for death row executions in the last 48 hours—"

Val's eyes stopped and just stared at the monitor. "My God!" she sighed.

Jake looked down at the screen and saw two photographs on the screen. Elisabeth Wheaton, 32, executed in Tempe, Arizona, six hours ago, and Reverend Morten Dublaise, executed 28 hours ago in Fairfax, Virginia.

"Dublaise, right here in our nation's capital. How convenient," noted Val.

"Convenient?" responded Jake. "This is beyond ironic. My God, we have one of the most brilliant cult leaders and mass murderers in the country, someone who makes Hannibal the Cannibal look like a saint, now inhabiting the body of the President. This guy has escaped the authorities for nearly thirty years using pure cunning and a chameleon's personality. He's made a career of taking on role after role."

"This is one of the greatest roles since Macbeth. We have to stop him. I have to get in to see Kovalik, evidence or no evidence."

Val was running the printouts of the FBI execution file as Jake was gathering all of his papers. They both knew what had to be done. Val was about to get her NSA emergency security call—the one she planted. A beeper page which would immediately bring her back to work and up close and personal with the security mainframe. That would allow her to track the intruder and of course cover her own tracks a little better.

Jake turned Val around on her computer office seat and gently held her face in his palms.

"Val, I love you. I have to get into Kovalik's office and deliver this evidence personally. I know we have evidence compelling enough to turn him to our side, but he has to read it. Now that he just got his best friend back, I'm not sure how accepting he'll be when I tell him the President is inhabited by the spirit of Dublaise—hell, I'd kick myself in the ass if someone brought this tall tale to me—but I have to try. Val, add this final piece of evidence to the e-mail bomb and launch it with a 24-hour fuse. If neither of us disarms it, it will be a last-ditch effort."

With a tender kiss, perhaps their last, Jake headed for the door.

17

THE PHOENIX

THE BODY OF President Sumner sat up in the hospital bed on the fifth floor of Walter Reed and looked around. Within the mind of Dublaise, the scene was somewhat surreal—but Dublaise was used to the surreal. He was used to apparitions and godly commandments. He was used to death and awakening. Most of all, he was an accomplished actor. Through his psychiatric and religious training, he was capable of mirroring other people's emotions. He could empathically feel confusion, joy, concern, and mirror the proper emotion back. That made him the perfect killer. No two people got the same sense from Dublaise. It was as if he was everything to everybody. That is why the FBI had such a difficult time tracking him down. He was no one person, but rather a mirror of what one wanted to see.

Officer Matthews immediately came to the bed as the President started stirring.

"Mr. President—my God, looks like you're OK. Can I get you anything?"

Dublaise remembered the execution, but things were a little cloudy now. Was this his personal hell? Things seemed much too sterile. And why was this guy calling him Mr. President? One thing he knew, however. He needed time. He needed to reach deeply into his resources. He needed to speak in generalities. It sounded like whoever or whatever he was now, he could use the shroud of confusion and disorientation.

Of an expected mental disorientation that would buy him time. He knew he desperately needed time.

"I am a little confused," responded Dublaise.

"That is certainly understandable, Mr. President. You were near death just 12 hours ago. I was there."

There was that word again—Mr. President. Could it be? Some sort of ironic joke? Perhaps a bizarre *Twilight Zone* episode. Dublaise slowly rubbed the inside of his hospital gown collar with his right forefinger, only to realize that the familiar creases and wrinkles of his neck felt different. His hand slowly rubbed his jaw, then drifted up to his cheeks and forehead. There was something wrong. Something different. One knows the feel of one's face. This was not his face!

His eyes gazed at the alarm clock by his bed. He looked at the digital date and time. Wednesday—he had lost over 24 hours since his execution on Monday! What was happening? He looked at Matthews' hospital security badge. He needed a name and familiarity. Calling this individual by his real name would immediately accomplish his task. He knew this intuitively. Everyone liked hearing their own name.

"Mr. Matthews, I am so glad to see you here. Can you help me to the bathroom?"

"Mr. President," replied Matthews with obvious conflict. Matthews was trained to take commands blindly from the President, but he was unsure if the President was allowed to get out of bed. Dublaise immediately sensed the conflict.

"Don't worry, I feel as strong as an ox. Just help me with this IV pole. A President can't take a dump in bed. It's unpatriotic," smiled Dublaise with just the right amount of eye contact. Matthews' positive and predictable response was immediate.

In the bathroom, Dublaise slowly turned to the sink and splashed cold water on his face. As he lifted his head to the mirror, an unusual feeling came over him. The reflection in the mirror was not his own. Handsome, many years younger, and completely alien. He patted his chest with both hands, as if to search for his heart—his soul. Whatever happened, this was a sign from God? A second chance?

A smirk came across his face as he looked at his reflection. "Hello, Lazarus—you have awakened from the dead," whispered Dublaise.

Once back in bed, he knew he had much work ahead. He needed to know what and how this happened. He recognized the face that looked back at him in the mirror. He was the President of the United States, but how and why? What a cosmic joke—a *Saturday Night Live* routine. He had to act swiftly. "Mr. Matthews, it seems that my memory of the last several days is very vague. You say I was near death and you were there. Please tell me what has happened."

Dublaise felt safe in asking such general questions. His loss of memory would certainly be understood and not questioned by Matthews. He needed access to other data with no time to waste. He knew that even the slightest mistake could be fatal in this chess game of life and death.

Matthews spent the next 90 minutes explaining what had happened. Dublaise sat there patiently, rubbing the inside of his pajama collar with his right forefinger. The story was more amazing than even Dublaise could believe. Dublaise knew the other side of the story. The side involving his own consciousness. Something was clearly overlooked by the Pentagon brain trust. This could not be the expected result of the MRI transfer scan. Oh, how Dublaise loved government bureaucracy!

He immediately surmised that they had made a pivotal mistake and did not know it. He knew that he was executed almost two days ago—or was he? He was now playing the Mephisto Waltz in the body of the President, and even the President's own bodyguard could not tell. He needed to find out more, but from whom?

What Dublaise did know was that he needed immediate access to information on President Sumner. His very survival depended on two things: immediate assumption of the President's personality and the immediate termination of anyone who could identify what had happened. The idiots obviously made a mistake. What were they thinking of?

"Matthews, thank you, but I tire somewhat easily. Please get me a laptop and a secure Internet connection. I want it within two hours. I need to get back in touch with the world. Of course I will need my Presidential security clearance. Can you arrange that?"

"Mr. President, I have a Think Pad with me. The hospital has a optical fiber line that is secure. I can have you on the Web in five minutes."

With those words, Dublaise knew he could pull this off. The last two years of cult activity had been heavily Web-focused. His church had one of the most sophisticated wide area networks in the country. All subversive activity was controlled via the exchange of information using 128-bit PGP security encoding. Even the FBI computers could not break the code. Dublaise was a true genius. He was as adept on the computer as he was in the pulpit.

Matthews set the computer up on the tray table, Ethernet cord plugged into an outlet next to the phone jack by the night table. The optical fiber line was 600 times faster than a conventional modem. Dublaise surfed the Web as if he had rockets strapped to his back. All that an outside observer would have seen was rapid flashing on the screen. He could photographically read and memorize pages as fast as they came up. He went through hundreds of official and unofficial websites dedicated to the President. President Sumner's youth, family relationships, Vietnam, early political campaigns, current policies, and friends. He intently read the popular lore surrounding the Purple Heart and Silver Star young Sumner got in Vietnam for saving Paul Kovalik. He committed an entire lifetime into memory in a brief two hours, all the while developing a psychological profile of the dead president. This would allow him to predict responses based on prior events.

The final piece was found in the National Archives. Dublaise had Level 1 presidential clearance. He could watch video feeds of all past presidential functions as well as some personal archived material from the History Channel containing private footage of the President. A little practice in front of the bathroom mirror, some vocal inflections, and even President Sumner's mother could not tell that anything was wrong.

Still, Dublaise knew that he needed to start off slow and feel the role. He knew he had little time, so he pushed himself to the limit. He fell asleep with the computer in front of him. By the time Dublaise passed out from sheer exhaustion, he had already breached the Pentagon and NSA presidential briefings on top-level security initiatives, and also penetrated Project Lazarus. He now understood!

General Kovalik looked in on his friend throughout the day, but this morning's rounds were a little more eventful. He could not wait to see David. The experiment was a success, and Kovalik had not slept for two days. This made him especially irritable when Jake burst through his front office that morning.

"I'm sorry, General!" cried the front secretary. "This guy just burst in and I couldn't stop him."

"That's all right, Mrs. Zelkewitz. I know this character. What brings you here, Jake? I understand you went AWOL last week. That breaks our deal. It's prison for you, my boy."

There was a certain gleam in Kovalik's eyes. He had a deep-seated anger that was difficult to understand. It had to do with entitlement and Jake's background. To Kovalik, Jake was a spoiled little shit who had genetically inherited too much brainpower and too little ethics. He was everything Kovalik despised in our society. Power with no discipline.

"General Kovalik, please give me a second. I know what you did with the President. Something is terribly wrong and I have the proof here. Please—just read it and then decide. All of our lives may depend on this."

Kovalik looked at the pile of documents Jake had dropped on the table and simultaneously depressed the Secret Security button under his desk. The MPs would burst in within a matter of seconds. Regardless of what Jake had to say, he needed to be contained immediately.

Jake heard the back door burst open and simultaneously saw two armed MPs running in side by side. Jake had no time to react. He immediately reverted back to his high school football days. As his coach used to say, "When you see a two rush defense, your instincts will tell you to run around the defenders, but if they are side by side, gun it up the middle!"

With that thought, Jake dashed at the door and burst through the guards. They were surprised by the rapid burst and even more surprised by Jake's flying elbows. By the time they could get up and pick up their Beretta 9 mm sidearms, Jake was down the hall, moving towards the South Wing stairwell.

"You get that son of a bitch!" shouted Kovalik as he threw all of Jake's papers onto the floor.

Jake ran through the stairwell at a breakneck pace, diving down the stairs five steps at a time, using the railings as his only means of support. He had this exit all planned, but he was hoping to at least get a word in edgewise with Kovalik before getting thrown out.

Right then, he realized that if he got caught he would never be able to prove his innocence.

He headed down through B1, the first of six basement levels. The morgue was on this level and exited directly on to a side entry ramp of Walter Reed. The ramp led to a small courtyard with a low brick wall. Jake and his friends used to get a little sauced on pure alcohol punch and often climbed the wall for fun after autopsy class. His immediate goal was to get out and over the wall—fun had nothing to do with it!

Jake's plan was simply to dash through the morgue and get into Bethesda traffic.

"Why is it that I'm always running down the corridors of this damn hospital?" mumbled Jake to himself as he rounded the corner leading past the autopsy suite.

Just as he rounded the corner, pursued by two armed guards from the rear, he heard the voices of at least two more guards approaching from the front. Trapped, he immediately backtracked and entered the only door available—the autopsy room.

Jake dashed into the room and looked around. He had to hide. Looking at the stainless steel doors along the wall, he quickly thought of hiding in the corpse storage bins. He briskly yanked the first door open—the bin occupied by a ripening MVA victim, face macerated and caved in, chest burst open by the impact of the steering wheel.

"Ugh! I'm wearing my seatbelt from now on," he remarked with his usual sarcasm. The gallows humor never leaves. It's the curse of Hippocrates.

Two more storage bins tried—full!

"Jesus Christ, people are dying to get in here. What the fuck is going on? I've got to get under cover!"

His last words were prophetic. Time was running out and within seconds, the main door burst open and two armed guards entered. The second guard turned, talking to the other two guards following. "You guys backtrack in case he went down the West corridor or into one of the labs. Get some backup. I think we have him cornered in this wing."

The first officer immediately went to the wall storage bins, opening each with flair. He pulled the doors open, yanked the stainless steel slabs out on their well-lubricated rollers, and then nearly simultaneously flipped the plastic cover off the

corpses with his left hand, cupping the underside of the gun
he was holding with his right hand in classic SWAT stance. For
a Walter Reed security guard, this was the most action he ever
saw. Besides, that's how Dirty Harry did it on the big screen.

Both guards then converged on the slab. That's what
everyone called the autopsy table. A corpse lay there, barely
covered. A half-dissected arm was hanging out of the sheet,
skin peeled off and muscles hanging, barely attached to the
bones.

This was medical student day, and dissecting a nonem-
balmed corpse was a special exercise. It was rare for students in
any school to practice on fresh cadavers. They jokingly called
it "fresh kill day" since most of the cadavers were victims of
the Washington "knife and gun club." It was interesting that
they all had the same name—John Doe.

The lead officer slowly approached the slab, which was
slightly angled towards the feet of the corpse. Although a
white plastic sheet covered most of the corpse, blood was
oozing down the sides of the pan towards the collecting sink
at the bottom of the slab. The officer slowly lifted the sheet
covering the dead man's face. Dirty Harry assumed his usual
pose, 9 mm semiautomatic in hand. The second officer lifted
the plastic sheet and both officers just stood there, paralyzed.

The scene would be difficult to witness for most nonmedical personnel. The corpse's face was completely dissected.
The right eye was exposed and pulled out of the orbital
socket. It was barely hanging off the side of the face by its
thin optic nerve. The round muscles surrounding the mouth
were exposed, giving the face an almost surreal expression.
The cranial vault was exposed in classic craniotomy fashion
and the skull dissection saw was lying just to the side of the
exposed and severed calvarium. The scalp and upper part of
the forehead was incised and peeled forward, partially covering the eyebrows but exposing the brain and its superficial
veins, arteries, and gyral pattern.

"This is fuckin' disgusting," remarked the lead officer. "There ain't nothing in here but stiffs. Let's get the hell out of here and help the others."

Dirty Harry couldn't answer. He was vomiting in the corner of the room, definitely not a classic police pose.

Jake heard the door shut but waited just a few more seconds to make sure the coast was clear. He felt disgusting. His body was in a fetal position, nestled and hidden between the legs of the corpse on the slab, his face pressed to the cold right thigh of the corpse, his entire right side drenched with the ooze and stench of blood and bodily fluids. The only thing protecting him from detection was the grotesque sight of the dissected cadaver. Jake knew that if they pulled the sheet down even twelve more inches, he would be found. It was not his first choice for a hiding place—it was his only choice.

He slowly crawled out from under the sheet and dropped straight to the floor, eyes peeking over the cadaver and at the door.

"Coast clear. Gotta get out of these clothes," he mumbled, looking at his blood-drenched outfit.

Jake lifted the half-dissected hand of the cadaver and shook it as a gentleman would shake the hand of a newly introduced social acquaintance. "Thank you, buddy," he said with a perfectly earnest expression. "You saved my ass."

Jake spotted a bin in the corner of the room, labeled "Hospital Scrub Uniforms." Most people called them scrubs. Jake called them a godsend. Within seconds, he used a moist towel to wipe himself down and got into fresh scrubs. Within minutes he was over the brick wall by the back ambulance entry ramp to the morgue and on the street outside of Walter Reed.

The guards were looking for him for the next four hours.

18

JEKYLL OR HYDE

PRESIDENT SUMNER RETURNED from the bathroom, dragging his intravenous pole back to the bed. He gently got back into the upright hospital mattress and started plugging at his laptop. The Web page he was looking at was entitled "The unauthorized Web biography of President David Sumner—things the White House does not want you to see!"

"Hello, Morten," spoke a deep voice in a dark corner of the room. "I approve of your reading list."

"Why, hello, Dr. Jones, I have been expecting you," responded Dublaise with a well-thought-out and purposeful inflection. "You are the only man on the Project Lazarus team that I could not explain. I do not like things that I cannot explain."

Jones was shocked at the response.

"You really didn't think someone with my history and intellect would just wake up as the President of the United States and not investigate? Thank God the government keeps such clear records of its own ineptitude."

How could that be? thought Abernathy. Could this man have processed all of the events within less than 24 hours?

"I assume you are unarmed, Dr. Jones, for I have already died once. But then again, you obviously know that. I had a sneaking suspicion that you did not belong on the team. Why would a Nobel Prize winner in physics participate in a medical experiment? Project Lazarus—interesting name."

Abernathy Jones was stunned. He needed time to think this through. There was no time. Dublaise had the advantage. The laptop on the President's table was connected to the State Department network and he had clearly used the Presidential security codes. The information Dublaise had, however was beyond the expected. He knew much, much more.

Jones slowly emerged from the shadows and the two men made eye contact. The only thing gleaming was a conspicuously large silver ring on Jones's middle finger bearing the bloodstone emblem of his Scottish clan.

The President's face now had a different look. One of intense focus and concentration. The eyes were those of Dublaise. Jones was a spiritual man, yet he was never fearful of the supernatural. He was now afraid.

"You know, Abernathy—I hope I can call you that? The government and the military act very much like the Church. Once you know the way, you can get anything you want because nobody knows it all. 'Need to know,' I believe you spook chaps call it."

"I have this incredibly loyal Secret Service chief outside, a Mr. Matthews. His job is to take a bullet for me, but as I talked to him, he seems to take things far more seriously. I do believe he would kill for me. He was there during the experiment, but neither he nor anyone else knew what really happened—at least that's the feeling I got from reading the NSA files on Project Lazarus.

"But you know what really happened, don't you, Abernathy?"

Somehow Jones got the distinct feeling he had played his trump card too early. He had thought he would have the upper hand, but Dublaise was in a different league. He now had no choice but to play the hand out, and Dublaise had the full house.

Dublaise just lay there smiling. "You know who I am, so the answer to my next question is very important to your future. If you bullshit me, I will make sure you never leave this building alive, and Mr. Matthews out there will make sure that even the NSA does not question your death!

"I strongly believe that three things motivate men: Fear, power and greed. I have but one question—*What do you want?*"

Abernathy stood there, initially staring into Dublaise's eyes. There was no more fear. He knew he was dealing with pure evil—the devil incarnate. He also knew he was about to sign the "contract." He was about to become the devil's advocate.

"I have pancreatic cancer. I was diagnosed two months ago. I have between six months and one year to live. Nobody knows!"

The pact was sealed with only four words. "I understand, my son."

It explained everything. Especially the unexplainable. Jake and Val could never have guessed. Abernathy's plan was as orchestrated as a Bohemian opera. The only thing missing was the characters. Although initially hard to conceive, Dublaise was the perfect partner to Jones. They both understood—no further words needed to be spoken.

Kovalik had no idea what possessed him even to glance at the volumes of paper Jake threw on his desk. He certainly knew that Jake was brilliant.

Something, however, made no sense. Why did Jake take the risk of coming to him--unless he had some compelling evidence? Something did not fit, and one thing made Kovalik worry—things that did not fit!

The documents were well prepared. The references and explanations were impeccable. He expected nothing less from Jake. Jake had got the largest NIH grant in the history of the Department of Radiology at MGH. What bothered Kovalik most was that Jake's data seemed to make sense. He read the

EEG patterns over and over. They seemed to hold the key. If the information proved correct, they were all screwed!

"Betty, do me a favor, STAT page Bill Perkins in neurology," said Kovalik into his intercom. Within minutes, Perkins came into the office.

"General, you paged me, sir?"

"At ease, Perkins," replied Kovalik. "You did a fellowship at Stanford on EEG interpretation, if my memory serves me correctly, did you not?"

"Yes, sir, I specialized in temporal seizure disorder."

"Never mind that bullshit," remarked Kovalik. "Can you discern patterns and personality profiles?"

"Yes, sir! That is integral to determining seizure activity."

Kovalik threw the EEG folders on the table and looked at Perkins sternly.

"This is top secret—do you understand? I want you to look at these patterns and do one thing—match the patients. I think a terrible mistake has been made and we may have inadvertently mixed some patients. Do you think you can do that in thirty minutes?" His tone made it a demand, not a request.

Kovalik then went to see President Sumner, his old friend. The journey to the presidential suite was somewhat uncomfortable. Kovalik did not necessarily want to know the answer. If he participated in the aberration of the century, his path was not to be a pleasant one, for not only would his best friend be dead, but he would be responsible for unleashing an evil beyond the comprehension of mortal man.

Kovalik opened the door to Sumner's room slowly. Matthews immediately glanced up and then went at ease. He recognized Kovalik. Dublaise looked up slowly, a strange cast of light shining on his youngish face from the laptop, still active and perched on his food tray.

Dublaise knew this was to be his first and most important test. He had studied the Peter Kovalik story intently, expecting this to be his first true test. If he could fake out his best friend, the rest would be easy.

"Peter, you're a sight for sore eyes," slowly commented Dublaise. He wanted to start the conversation, but keep it minimal and relatively vague.

"David, you gave us quite a scare."

He was cautious and reserved enough that Dublaise picked up on the hesitancy immediately. That was Dublaise's forte, the ability to read the unsaid. The ability to discern an entire tale from but one glance. He immediately knew he had to score with Kovalik. He had to rapidly gain his confidence. It was too early, but Kovalik's eyes told him he had to take a gamble.

"Matthews told me what you did, Paul. You saved my life and I am grateful. Just like in Nam, but the shoe is on the other foot, hey, buddy?" smiled Dublaise. The reference to the camaraderie they felt for each other in Nam was bound to negate all suspicion—or so he thought!

Kovalik's expression did indeed change, but not to one of comfort. The transition was so intense and so transparent that Dublaise needed no special skills to see the faux pas.

"David," responded Kovalik with a sense of uncomfortable urgency. "I'm glad you're looking better. Consider us even for Nam!" Peter Kovalik left without making eye contact. He awaited no further pleasantries. He had his answer. He did not need Perkins's EEG interpretation.

Kovalik now knew this was not President Sumner. In the twenty-seven years since Viet Nam, Sumner had never spoken of his heroics. The press and dignitaries would continually bring it up, to the same negative response. To bring this sensitive topic up in such a gratuitous manner was beyond uncharacteristic. This was not David Sumner.

19

STRANGE BEDFELLOWS

BACK IN HIS office, Kovalik finished rereading Jake's documentation, including the reference to the pending e-mail bomb. Kovalik's fury was nearly uncontrollable. He had to find Jake before the e-mail bomb was sent to every government agency and newspaper under the sun.

"God, I hate fucking amateurs!" yelled Kovalik as Perkins entered the office.

"General Kovalik," muttered Perkins. "I finished the EEG interpretations, sir—how did you know?"

"What?"

"The names, sir! The findings were very subtle and were only seen in the frontal lobe, but I believe that there is a mistake in the names. Some of the repeating patterns clearly belong to the other patients in the folder you showed me."

Kovalik's anger was cut like a knife by that statement. It brought him back to reality and the task at hand. Perkins was military, and he was a good doctor. This was no time for anger. This was time for professionalism.

Kovalik realized what he needed to do. He was an Army Ranger, trained to think under adverse conditions and kill under ALL conditions. It was now time to plan.

"Thank you, Perkins," responded Kovalik with controlled inflection. "This conversation never happened—dismissed!"

Back on the ward, Abernathy came out from behind the opaque curtains covering the south window to the presidential suite. Matthews did not even budge as Jones approached the President. He understood that Abernathy Jones was an insider. That was all he needed to know. Who to protect and who to kill—a rather simple job.

Matthews worked in Costa Rica for four years as a CIA operative. That was a fancy word for assassin. After he had "sanctioned" seven drug cartel leaders, his superiors brought him in. He worked some small jobs for the NSC and FBI. When the director of the Secret Service came across his file while preparing for a presidential visit to Chile, Matthews' qualities jumped out. Nobody knew South America better than Matthews, and nobody could follow orders better—without question. After the escort job, Matthews was enlisted into Secret Service training school. He had the exceptional combination of a high IQ, loyalty, and no remorse or regard for personal safety. The rest was history. Matthews was the best, because he simply did not give a shit about anything other that the President.

"Matthews, Dr. Jones and I need some privacy. Would you wait outside the door?" requested Dublaise, nervously rubbing the inside of his collar with his right forefinger.

Matthews simply got up and left without any change in expression. His loyalty was unshakeable. The man in front of him was President Sumner.

"He knows," said Abernathy. "Kovalik knows you are not the President. You said something, I don't know what. You said something that triggered him."

"He suspected," responded Dublaise. "I could tell from the moment he entered the room. He needed some sort of confirmation and I inadvertently gave it to him. I won't make that mistake again."

"Now what?" asked Abernathy.

"The Lord giveth, and the Lord taketh away," replied Dublaise. "We shall prepare first by taking power ourselves, then by taking it away from our enemies. Can you handle a gun, Dr. Jones?"

"Although I am a nuclear physics professor, one does not work in the Weapons Division of the Pentagon without learning how to handle the more conventional firearms. As a matter of fact, in my youth I could outshoot a few of our finest. I must say, I actually carried a snub-nosed .38 on some of my ghost-busting adventures. Silly, isn't it?"

"My, you are full of surprises, Abernathy? This time, however, your potential targets will not be apparitions," said Dublaise with a decidedly evil smile and low laugh.

Abernathy turned and left the room. Upon leaving, he could think only one thought: "At what price this pact with the devil? At what price?"

Abernathy Jones was indeed a multifaceted individual. A man of incredible brilliance, yet of spiritual unrest. World War II was a turning point for many a young man in America. Jones was beginning his thesis on black holes at MIT when he decided to take a six-month sabbatical at Princeton to study under a relatively unknown theoretician named Guggenheim. That six-month period enlightened and developed his mathematical mind even beyond that of his teacher. He saw subtle faults in even Einstein's logic, faults which when solved would eventually earn Jones a Nobel Prize.

Back in MIT, the State Department was scouring our greatest universities for physicists. That was when Jones was introduced to the NSA and Pentagon. He found that with just a little cooperation, he could get anything he wanted—a laboratory, unlimited research funds, and, most importantly, anonymity. Even his wife did not know of his government projects. Just that his research took him to Los Alamos, New Mexico, every once in a while because they had the world's largest cyclotron.

Ghost busting came much later in Jones's career. The news that his wife had ovarian cancer came nearly coincidentally with his Nobel Prize nomination. His internal turmoil was devastating. At the cusp of his master physics achievement he suffered the loss of the only thing that mattered in his life. He had no children, no legacy—just Natalie.

Natalie died exactly one day after her husband received his honor in Stockholm. She held on, and then she just let go.

Her death was truly Abernathy's turning point. "I shall never leave you, my darling Abernathy. No matter where you are, I shall be right next to you" were the neatly written words next to her deathbed.

The next two years were a blur to Jones. He started experimenting with the origin of static magnetic fields. He went to every priest, rabbi, shaman, and spiritualist he could find. Of course, most of the séances he attended were frauds; however, he believed in one thing. The human spirit can remain on this plane we call mortal existence. Einstein was right, $E = mc^2$, and E stood for magnetic energy in the case of ghosts. That is why the EM flux meters always went off when a spirit was in the room. Jones had no doubt.

Was it strange that a Nobel Prize winner believed in the spiritual? Was it strange that Abernathy Jones was a ghost hunter? No, because he was not searching for ghosts. He just wanted to say goodbye to his wife. She had died just moments before his return from Stockholm. He was not there when she passed.

Abernathy just wanted to say goodbye.

20

PLAN B

JAKE WALKED INTO the apartment looking even worse than before. He smelled like a dissection experiment gone wrong, his body stained with the blood and bodily fluids of the cadaver he just nestled with. The thought made him sick, but the sight made Val even sicker. Jake's hair was caked with blood and slicked down the side of his face.

"Jake, every time you walk through the door you look worse," said Val. "I don't think your body can take another journey without you going through the magnet yourself."

Although it was funny in a macabre sort of way, Jake had no more energy left. This was the end of his rope. "Kovalik was his usual charming self," he said. "Val, we have to do it."

"It—what is it?" questioned Val. "So far we broke into Walter Reed twice, I used my security ID, allowing a direct trace, I hacked into the Pentagon computer, we stole classified documents, I doctored NSA records, and you are AWOL with some serious federal charges and a national warrant. At this rate, the only thing we haven't done is to kill the President of the United States."

Jake looked at Val without expression and simply shook his head. Val's response was a blank stare and disbelief.

"Val, we have to. We have nothing more to lose. Kovalik was our last chance," responded Jake with a regretful tone. "I have a gun. My Dad gave it to me when I moved to the city.

I have to get in to Walter Reed one more time and kill the President. You have to make sure the e-mail gets out."

"Right, Jake!" yelled Val. "Let me think this through. You are going to take a loaded gun, march it into Walter Reed knowing that your face is on every security billboard in the institution and probably on the FBI's most wanted list, walk into the presidential suite past the Secret Service, and blow away the President. Even if you get that far, Jake, you won't make it out alive. My e-mail bomb won't protect a dead man. No, you're fucking out of your mind. Besides, Jake, I've been reading up on Morten Dublaise. This guy is smart and paranoid. By this time, if he's fooled Kovalik, he's probably set up his defensive net. This guy has been on the run for almost thirty years. He makes *very* few mistakes."

"You're right, Val," responded Jake after some more thought. "We need a plan we can survive."

Their ultimate plan was quite simple, but took two hours to develop. All the while, Kovalik was back at Walter Reed, staring at the picture on his wall of him and David Sumner—buddies in Nam.

Kovalik's intercom rang. "Dr. Kovalik, it's the FBI."

Kovalik picked up the phone. "Yeah, this is General Kovalik—no—no, it was just a local intrusion. Nothing to do with the President. As I told the Secret Service boys, just an unrelated wacko. I'm personally taking care of it. Call the bulldogs off!"

Kovalik hung the phone up with his usual authority. He had just bought himself some needed time to find Jake. If the spooks found him first, it would be curtains for everyone.

Then it dawned on him. He and Jake had the same mission now. The President needed to die. Jake would come back. He had to. Kovalik just had to wait and Jake would come to him. He just needed to stop Jake before he made a stupid mistake. "Betty, could you come in here?"

"Yes, General," answered his secretary as she entered his office.

"He can't be working alone," thought Kovalik to himself. "I need to find his accomplice. It has to be someone with security clearance."

"Betty, call security and have them go through the T-6 tapes for the last four days—and also the main lobby tapes. Tell them to cross-reference them with the photo ID of Jake Eriksson. If any suspicious characters even vaguely resembling Eriksson entered the building, I want the pictures. Tell them he entered with an accomplice and it's their asses if the photos are not on my desk in thirty minutes."

The pictures were on his desk in twenty-three minutes—two figures dressed in scrubs. Jake's profile was difficult to ID, but Val's face was a direct frontal shot.

"Well, this explains it all," smiled Kovalik. "Jake and our little Miss NSA Security. Now I know the prey shall come to the hunter!"

Back at the apartment, Jake and Val were finalizing their plans.

"Let's go through this again," stated Jake while going down a scribbled list on a yellow legal pad. "The Walter Reed records tell us that the President gets a low-dose Lovinox shot in his IV every four hours. We changed the ID of the call nurse to one with your picture using your security access. You will pick it up from the security desk so that you can access the President's suite. You enter the building and tell security that you lost your ID and pick up a duplicate copy on the first floor. At the same time, we change the shift of the original nurse and tell her to come in two hours later for a ten-hour shift to cover someone else."

"Got it," responded Val with due trepidation.

"At the same time, I'm parked outside the side entry, next to the morgue. There's usually no traffic there. Like the roach motel—they go in but nobody comes out," smiled Jake. Val didn't smile back. She had heard that one at least twice before.

"Val, you'll be carrying pure KCl in a 10cc syringe in your right sleeve. Go to the presidential suite, check in with the Secret Service and show your ID. Explain that the duty nurse got sick and you are her call replacement. Pick up the President's chart. The first page will have the medication list. Just initial the lowest entry, walk over to the med cart, pick up a tray, and look at the little drawers. Take out one syringe labeled Lovinox and put it on the tray. As you walk down the hall, pull the switch—slip the Lovinox into your sleeve and place the KCl on the tray. When you see the President, make some pleasant conversation, but be quick and businesslike. Swipe the IV port on the tubing from the pole once with an alcohol swipe turn the IV off; you don't want to alert suspicion by not using sterile technique.

"Then rapidly inject the KCL and turn the IV wide open. Just leave and keep on walking. Don't turn around or look back. He should go into cardiac arrest within 20 seconds. Bells will go off and an immediate crash team response will burst in. The Code Blue will cause enough confusion for you to get way."

Val stared at Jake nervously. She was scared out of her mind, but there was no other way out. They were both in deep trouble, and the whole world was in even deeper trouble. They could not even conceive of Dublaise as leader of the world's strongest nuclear power. Dublaise's history was the preaching of the destruction and rebirth of the world—the fox was now guarding the henhouse.

21

PLAN A

VAL ENTERED WALTER Reed wearing a very attractive white nurse's uniform they had picked up at the local uniform supply store, three blocks away from the hospital. Jake used a syringe from his doctor's bag and purchased some potassium chloride at a local hobby shop. The mixture was easy—he certainly didn't need to worry about sterility!

Val's entry was uneventful, as the Walter Reed lobby was enormous and filled with people. After stopping at the security desk to pick up her "lost" ID badge, she flashed her nurse's badge nonchalantly at the main reception desk, briefly glancing at the camera immediately above the head of the guard officer. As she rounded the corner to enter the South Wing elevator bank, two officers briskly grabbed her, one on each arm. The officer to her right bent down to whisper in her ear.

"Dr. Kovalik is waiting for you in security. Please come quietly!"

Kovalik watched the scene on the security monitors and smiled. He knew his trap would work. His men had her picture posted at every monitoring post.

"Hello, there, Valerie, is it?" asked Kovalik with a very serious and businesslike look on his face. "I am sure the NSC and your boss will be interested in the tapes we have of your after-hours activities."

Kovalik slapped about a dozen prints from various observational cameras. Val looked at the pictures and said nothing. They could clearly identify both her and Jake. It was over.

Within minutes, two more armed guards entered the room, holding Jake in handcuffs. Jake's guards did not look as pleasant as her escorts.

"Well, what do we have here?" smirked Kovalik. "Is it Bonnie and Clyde or Butch and Sundance? More like Bonnie and Clyde. You know, Miss Valerie, you have a striking resemblance to Faye Dunaway."

Val looked away. Somehow she did not find this tête-à-tête amusing.

"Look, Kovalik, you have us. I know my rights," Jake blurted out. "We get a lawyer and a phone call. You get to leave us the fuck alone!"

"Listen, asshole!" responded Kovalik. "You *have* no rights. You and your girlfriend breached this federal institution at least three times. You falsified documents, entered a Black Level confined area, and odds have it that the syringe we found on your girlfriend does not contain insulin for her chronic diabetes, get the drift? We need a serious pow-wow here. Let's go!"

The security officers immediately rose to attention as Kovalik got up. "Take the cuffs off this asshole," Kovalik told the senior officer. "He's only dangerous to himself."

They left the security office expecting to go to the brig or to the garage for processing at Langley, but Kovalik pushed the second floor button in the elevator, which led to the Administration Wing, definitely a low-security area. When Jake turned around in the elevator, he noticed that guards were gone and it was only Kovalik and Val behind him. Could this be their chance?

"Should I try to hit Kovalik and make another run for it with Val?" thought Jake to himself.

"Now don't do anything dumb, Jake," said Kovalik, as if reading his mind. "I'm a trained Ranger and can probably break your neck with one move. The building is covered, and before you do anything rash, you are both going to want to hear what I am about to say."

They walked into Kovalik's office and sat down, Kovalik behind his desk, Jake and Val nervously sitting in the two chairs immediately in front of the massive oak desk. Kovalik started fiddling with the large pile of papers Jake had left, pulling out the EEG strips.

"You were right all along, Jake. I had these EEGs looked at by one of our experts. They did not go into as much detail as you did. However, the results were essentially identical to your notes. We are transferring the entire being, aren't we?" asked Kovalik with a saddened look.

"Yes," responded Jake.

"You know, Jake, we really are quite similar, and I admit I never gave you a break. All I saw was a rich, spoiled young man who was raised with a silver spoon in his mouth. I guess I also did some brash things in my youth and my modesty was perhaps a work-in-progress. Probably still is, according to my wife. You really are quite brilliant. Your plans this time were, however, quite foolish."

"What made you change your mind, General?" asked Val. "I doubt that you would trust the EEGs alone."

"You're right, Valerie. It's the President—or whatever abomination I created. You see, we went to Nam together. It got real hot and heavy and I was trapped behind enemy lines. The story has been retold about a thousand times. President Sumner hated that story, because he got the Congressional Medal of Honor and Silver Star and he thought I deserved it. Mind you, he saved my ass and I was first to shake his hand, but a lot of grunts did heroic things like that without getting the medal. David's father, the Senator, had it all planned."

"So what's that got to do with today?" asked Jake.

"When I went upstairs, the man pretending to be the President boasted about Nam—he said we were 'now even.'

In 27 years, the "real" David would not mention saving my life, publicly or privately. He would never bring it up, Never! This is not David Sumner and we have to kill him!"

The words were a shock to both Jake and Val. They finally had an ally, someone on the inside they could trust. Kovalik took the syringe out of his pocket and placed it on the table. "I assume this is KCL," he said.

"One hundred percent," answered Jake. "Guaranteed to induce a fatal heart block within twenty seconds."

Kovalik opened his bottom drawer and pulled out a 9 mm H&K semi automatic pistol, the kind used by Special Ops. He pulled back the top of the barrel and chambered a round into the gun by snapping the slide forward. Kovalik then slammed the gun on the table. The noise startled both Jake and Val.

"And if the KCL doesn't stop his heart, a 9 mm round will!" continued Kovalik with a look rarely seen on the face of mortal men. Kovalik had last felt like this in Vietnam, grenade under his left shoulder blade. He had nothing to lose. He owed this to David. He owed this to his nation.

"That's suicide," remarked Val.

"No, Valerie, allowing Morten Dublaise to run this country and control our nuclear arsenal is suicide. Your plan is suicide. You wouldn't have gotten within thirty feet of the President. I see how Dublaise has been acting. He already suspects everyone—perhaps even me. His Secret Service act like Caesar's Praetorian Guards, and the lead agent would as soon kill you as ask questions.

"Within a few days, Dublaise will have studied enough tapes and will have read enough about Sumner that even David's wife would not be able to tell the difference. He won't make this same mistake again, and once he finds out about his faux pas, I'm dead anyway.

"I'll try to inject the KCL first. Tonight, when the staff is on skeleton shift and only his guard is there, I'll go in and access the IV. If something goes wrong, the H&K in my waistband will be my backup—loaded and ready to shoot."

Jake looked at Kovalik through different eyes now. Here was a man of conviction and honor. A man who came up the hard way and lived through the horrors of war, yet still was willing to make the ultimate sacrifice. Jake just stood up and in his best military form, executed a perfect Marine salute. "An honor to serve with you, sir!" he snapped.

"Now don't get military on me, you little snot-nosed rich boy. I just think your talent and your pretty little girlfriend won't serve our country well from behind bars," smiled Kovalik.

They spent the next hour planning the attack and escape. Val described the e-mail bomb in detail, including the deactivation sequence. Jake went through his papers, word for word, including their meeting with Abernathy Jones. Kovalik immediately looked up at hearing the name.

"Jones—Jones—the nuclear physics guy," mumbled Kovalik.

"Yes," responded Jake, curious as to why that would ring a bell with Kovalik. "How do you know him?"

"I occasionally get invited to Pentagon briefings as the President's medical liaison. He always wanted to give me a high-ranking cabinet position, but I've resisted it like the plague. Anyway, I went to a meeting on development of antipersonnel plasma weapons capable of working both on earth and in space. They had a cadaver demonstration in a vacuum and David wanted my medical opinion. Abernathy Jones was the lead physicist. Then he mysteriously gets shoved down my throat and gets top security BlackIce clearance to Project Lazarus. When I tried to stop it, I got my ass kicked by the Pentagon brass!"

"What?" asked Val, somewhat irritated. "General, you're rambling. What does this have to do with Dublaise and the President's body?"

"He was there at the controls during the President's MRI transfer. This is bad. If you tell me you told Jones about your suspicions and Jones is now involved with the President, something is wrong—something is very wrong. He wanted to be there when Dublaise's soul got transferred. He would not leave and pulled security rank on me."

Val and Jake looked at each other. It finally made sense to them also. They could never understand why Jones refused to help them when they obviously had the answers and evidence he needed. They presented him with a ghost-hunter's dream and he backed away—or did he?

"They know and are planning together," continued Kovalik. "We have to regroup our forces and prepare for the serious contingency of complete failure. Tonight is the night! Valerie, we must send the e-mail bomb now, but we must change the distribution list. Can you send it to the NSC now and to the rest of the recipients automatically tomorrow—unless of course we override the code and all goes well?"

"Sure," responded Val with a look of confusion. "I don't know what you are getting at. Why send to the NSC now?"

"Failsafe," responded Kovalik. "If we get caught, Dublaise is bound to override all of our codes. I'm sure he is already hunting you both. That's why you would have never made it. This way, no matter what, the NSA will have all of the data and if anything happens to us, they will activate Seal Team Zero."

"What the hell is Seal Team Zero?" asked Jake, somewhat dizzy at this turn of events.

"Seal Team Zero does not exist! Let me make that clear. Its mission, however, is to assassinate the President of the United States or any other high-ranking official in the case of what is called an 'imperative breach.' It answers only to the NSC and only with Joint Chiefs' primary approval."

Somehow it all made sense to Jake. Most governments must have such a tactical team. It's just that nobody can admit to it.

Within seconds, Val logged on to Kovalik's computer and the e-mail bomb went out. They were now locked into the plan. With a click of a button, Val sent the e-mail bomb to the first set of recipients—"failsafe."

Kovalik next made some high-level calls. The first call was to the Judge Advocate General of the Armed Forces.

"Yeah, Frank—that's right—Jake Eriksson—all charges dropped. No, I don't want anything on his record other than an honorable discharge. Actually, make that an honorable discharge with high commendation. I want the charges to disappear, we found out the alcohol test and pacemaker thing was a mistake—my grunts accessed data on the wrong patient—very embarrassing for Walter Reed. Fax me the documents right now for signatures, I may be going out of town."

Jake and Val just watched with wonder as call after call was made. The power Kovalik had was incredible. Doors would swing open or shut at the mere inflection of his voice. The next call was even more unusual.

"Hello, Vance," said Kovalik with a little wink directed towards Val. "This is Paul Kovalik. How the hell are you? Margie still playing tennis? Good—good—listen, I have a favor to ask of you. Do you still have that opening for the Section Head of Neuroradiology at McMaster in Montreal? No shit, great! Well I have this Harvard-trained neuroradiologist here at Walter Reed. Great guy—you would do well by him. I owe his daddy a few favors, if you know what I mean. Anyway, he's terrific even without the pull, but you have to get me out of this jam. Yeah, I'll send him up tomorrow for an interview. I owe you *big*!"

Kovalik then immediately pressed the intercom button to talk to his secretary. "I need two airplane tickets from here to Montreal for tonight. Use my special military clearance. If we can't go commercial, we'll send a transport to out there with medical supplies for our Montreal base hospital. Be creative, Betty. I want federal FBI clearance and no names on the tickets and set them out on my Pentagon account. Label it Nicaragua." Kovalik turned to Jake and covered the telephone mouthpiece. "Nobody in the Pentagon questions any charge labeled Nicaragua. It's like the herpes of the military."

The plan was set and relatively simple. Jake and Val were to get out of the hot zone and Canada was as safe as anywhere on earth. If the plan were successful, Val would confirm the President died on the news and send the abort code from the airport on her wireless laptop modem. Kovalik would take care of the NSC and Joint Chiefs. Jake was already set with a dream academic job, out of sight in Canada. Val would be magically transferred to the Canadian branch of the State Department, where she could continue her present work—and handle any necessary computer cleanup.

If the plan was a failure, they were already on the way to Canada. The rest would be up to them—and destiny. They would be fugitives with a twenty-four-hour head start. Better odds than they had in DC!

In the President's room, Morten Dublaise was getting ready to go to sleep when his now specially configured laptop flashed a large red sign: "URGENT TOP SECRET MESSAGE—EYES ONLY—NATIONAL SECURITY COUNCIL."

It was the e-mail bomb. Dublaise was already monitoring all security traffic.

22

MEXICAN STANDOFF

KOVALIK CALLED TWO cabs and Jake and Val went to their respective apartments to pack. Their exit was to be rapid, but they needed clothes and toiletries for at least two weeks. They emptied their accounts of cash and took all of their credit cards. They arrived nearly simultaneously at Washington's Reagan International Airport for a 10:45 commercial flight to Montreal.

Walter Reed was fairly slow and dark at night. The military doctors were not known for putting in long hours. The elevator to the presidential suite was private. All of the guards immediately recognized Kovalik and stood at attention as he walked by. He visited the President often enough not to attract any undue attention and he certainly would not be searched.

Kovalik approached the President's room with more than the usual attentiveness. Matthews was outside the door, reading *Time Magazine*. He barely moved as Kovalik went by, but that was his training. If you asked him one month later, he would be able to tell you what color pants and what type of shoes Kovalik wore. As Kovalik entered the room, he saw the President partially reclined in his hospital bed, asleep with the TV broadcasting the local news. The glare from the screen eerily shone on the face of his former best friend. Could he go through with the plan? Kovalik paused for a long while, just staring. Maybe they were all wrong. How could he live with himself if he made a mistake?

No. The data were all there and confirmed. This was not David Sumner. This was a carcass inhabited by Morten Dublaise, the serial killer and cult murderer of the century. Kovalik went on—he had to.

Immediately to the right of the president was an IV pole holding a 250 cc bottle of saline with some vitamin supplements. The IV had a central access port for medication, tubing leading to the President's right arm. They were going to take the IV out prior to discharge in the morning.

Slowly, with quiet and deliberate steps, Kovalik approached the President, KCL syringe in hand. He slowly unbuttoned the bottom of his lab coat, exposing the H&K—just in case.

Kovalik briskly uncapped the syringe and picked up the access port to the IV with his left hand. As he was about to plunge the syringe into the port with his thumb, a hand grabbed his wrist, nearly breaking his carpal bones. The IV pole crashed to the floor with a high-impact shatter. It was Dublaise's hand, now powerfully twisting Kovalik's right arm and keeping the KCL from ending his perverse life a second time.

Kovalik untwisted his arm, simultaneously dropping the syringe on the floor and drawing the 9 mm H&K from his waist. He pointed it right at Dublaise's head.

"It's not going to go as easily for me as I thought," said Kovalik, staring into the eyes of Dublaise. He now saw right through his outer façade. These were the eyes of a mass murderer, not his friend. "But at the end," he said out loud, "justice will be served."

"Paul, you were the only one who could trap me," smiled Dublaise. "Everyone else would be inconsequential. I have been expecting you."

"Drop the gun, General Kovalik," said the deep voice of Abernathy Jones, emerging from behind the curtain, holding a gun directly to Kovalik's temporal lobe. Abernathy's Celtic silver ring shone brightly underneath the butt of the silver .38 Special revolver.

Nearly simultaneously Matthews burst through the hospital door, gun drawn and pointing at the scene. Matthews started swinging the gun first at Jones, then Kovalik, and then Jones again. He couldn't decide who the bad guy was. Dublaise started laughing uncontrollably. "Why, I believe this is called a good old Mexican standoff!"

It was the type of sarcastic laughter often heard in Shakespearian tragedies. The type of laughter Macbeth projected the moment prior to his reckoning.

The laughter ended with a single bang and a bright muzzle flash, disrupting the eerie darkness of the Walter Reed presidential suite.

23

THE MORNING AFTER

JAKE AND VAL nervously awaited their flight in the National Airport bar, she sipping on a glass of California Merlot and he on his favorite amber ale. They made little conversation. Val asked the bartender to change the TV channel to CNN. He refused, choosing instead to watch his favorite rerun of *M*A*S*H*. The longest hour of their lives passed with excruciating anxiety. If they got no message before boarding, Kovalik failed and the e-mail bomb would automatically send.

Moments before the preflight boarding call, all of the television sets in the bar changed to a solemn-faced anchorman—

"We interrupt your normally scheduled program for this emergency broadcast from the White House—"

A cut to the external view of a brightly lit White House façade immediately followed an interior view in the pressroom. The President's Chief of Staff briskly walked on to the podium.

"At 11:32, I received an emergent call from General Paul Kovalik, Chief of Staff of the Walter Reed Army Medical Center, informing me of a second and this time fatal stroke suffered by President David Sumner. All attempts at saving the President failed. He was pronounced dead of natural causes at 11:22. May God have mercy on his soul—"

Tears welled up in the eyes of many of the onlookers. Without feeling, Val opened her laptop and activated her wireless modem, simultaneously logging onto her e-mail account in the Pentagon. She found her e-mail and typed DEACTIVATE PROJECT—code:/LAZARUS. When prompted, she typed the password TANTALUS. They then boarded the plane with no time to spare, never looking back.

Montreal was a lovely place to live. Jake not only got the job of head of neuroradiology of one of the most prestigious institutions in the world, but also became nationally published with grants in early tumor detection with MRI. Val quit her State Department job after finishing some of her outstanding assignments and started a computer consulting firm specializing in network security and hacker prevention. Microsoft was her largest client. She could support them both on the money she made in one month working for some of the top computer companies in the world. "It takes the best to beat the best in the hacker world," Val always said.

One year after their fateful flight from DC, Val was expecting their first baby. Jake was obsessed. He ultrasounded her at least once a week—just to make sure. It was a boy! Val hoped it possessed as few of Jake's genes as possible, but all in all the little fella could have done worse—and so could she. They were very much in love.

They lived in a remote community, overlooking a lake just north of Montreal. Mornings were an especially cherished time for them. They would sip on that wonderful first morning cup of coffee while watching the mist rise off the lake.

Jake was listening to his son's heartbeat, head pressed against Val's protruding stomach. He could hear nothing; the TV was too loud. As he got up to turn the volume down, his eyes stared at the screen in disbelief.

He recognized the figures on the screen. The scene was a press room and the speaker was General Paul Kovalik. To his side was James Matthews, the President's ex-Secret Service agent. The camera focused on the face of Kovalik.

"I make this announcement with a heavy heart, but a spirit of enthusiasm. It has been one year since David Sumner, our President, my colleague, and my closest friend, tragically died. It has been a year of soul-searching and personal unrest. I realized that this unrest shall only come to an end when I fulfill the personal vow I made to David Sumner on his death bed—and that is to continue his work, his dreams, and make this country better four years from now than it has ever been."

"I hereby officially announce my candidacy for the President of this wonderful nation."

As the TV camera backed up to pan the press room, a brief flash of light reflected on the camera lens from a large silver ring on the right forefinger of James Matthews, bearing the crest and bloodstone of the Jones clan.

Kovalik ended the press conference with an undeniable look of confidence, slowly rubbing the inside of his collar with his right forefinger.

EPILOGUE

The Wall Street Journal, **September 23, 2002**

Medical Magnetics (NASD-MMI) Stock Plummets amid Massive Selloff Following Surprise FDA Licensure Denial of New Super-Powered MRI Magnet. *By Hajid Rammanpour, Staff Reporter, The Wall Street Journal.*

In a surprise FDA move, clinical trials involving the T-6 superconductive MRI magnet were halted due to "insufficient clinical evidence guaranteeing the safety of patients in an ultrahigh magnetic field." Lead investigators in three current installations, including the University of Pennsylvania, Stanford, and the Walter Reed Army Medical Center, declined to comment, noting that the magnet is currently under investigation and all data are highly confidential.

Medical Magnetics (MMI), a startup company founded by lead researchers from Bell Labs and General Electric Medical, designed the first magnet capable of generating magnetic fields over 400,000 times the magnetic pull of the earth and over five times the strength of any existing medical MRI magnet. Early research showing superior tumor visualization and actual tumor growth factor inhibition sparked Wall Street and induced one of the fastest corporate growth spurts in history. Awaiting almost certain FDA approval, 130 units were ready for shipment worldwide when the FDA ruling hit this morning.

During an immediate press conference, Gunther Warhol, CEO of Medical Magnetics, attempted to stave off market reaction.

"To our knowledge, over 500 patients in three prominent medical centers safely underwent MRI exams with not only improved tumor visualization, but actual induced remission. We do not understand the basis of the FDA ruling and will certainly appeal it. The medical community has embraced this technology and it should not be kept from the public."

Inside sources in the FDA unofficially stated that the termination of the T-6 trials was ordered "from the highest level, based on scientific concern." Our sources stated that the decision was unlikely to be overturned.

ABOUT THE AUTHOR

Edward Steiner, MD, graduated Phi Beta Kappa from Harpur College in 1978 with a Bachelor's Degree in Biology. Following his undergraduate studies, he entered the University of Rochester School of Medicine, where he received his MD. After completing an Internship in General Surgery, Dr. Steiner completed his Radiology Residency at Strong Memorial Hospital/University of Rochester Medical Center. He was named chief resident in 1985 and was accepted as a Fellow in Interventional Radiology/Body Imaging at Harvard Medical School/ Massachusetts General Hospital. In his two years at Harvard, he was promoted to Clinical Assistant Radiologist in 1986 and published over twenty-three journal articles, reviewed two texts for national journals, wrote two book chapters, and presented thirteen scientific papers at national meetings.

Dr. Steiner pioneered research and clinical trials in the deployment of metallic devices inside the human body for the treatment of cancer patients. He is currently a national lecturer in Interventional Radiology and Medical Information Technology, and Chief of Radiology at Sinai Hospital of Baltimore.

"The most impressive element of this book (Soul Survivor) was the way you parlayed your obvious medical knowledge into a commercial suspense setting. The backdrop was very credible, something that is often lacking in 'medical thrillers.'"

—Jason Kaufman, Senior Editor, The Doubleday Broadway Publishing Group, A Division of Random House